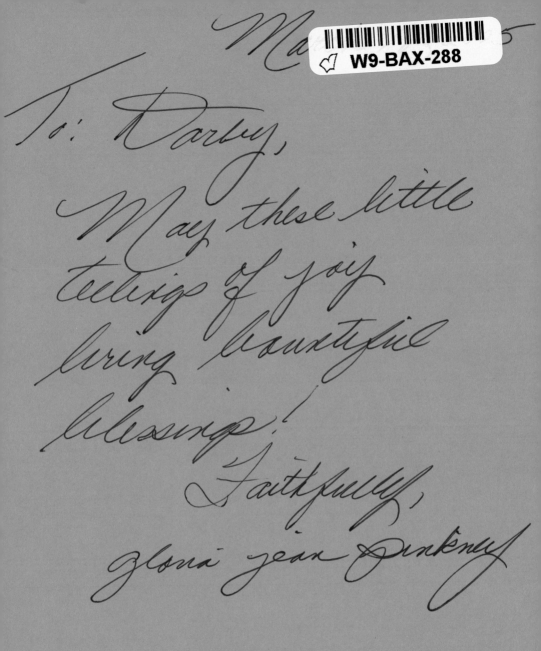

Ma...

To: Darby,

May these little
feelings of joy
bring beautiful
blessings!

Faithfully,
gloria jean pinkney

In the Forest of Your Remembrance

"Blessed is she who believed,
for there will be a fulfillment of those things
which were told her from the Lord."

LUKE 1:45
(NKJV)

In the Forest of Your Remembrance

Thirty-three Goodly News Tellings for the Whole Family

Gloria Jean Pinkney

For God so loved the world that
He gave His only begotten Son, that
whoever believes in Him should not
perish but have everlasting life.

JOHN 3:16 (NKJV)

Illustrations by Jerry Pinkney,
Brian Pinkney, and Myles C. Pinkney

PHYLLIS FOGELMAN BOOKS · NEW YORK

Published by Phyllis Fogelman Books
An imprint of Penguin Putnam Inc.
345 Hudson Street
New York, New York 10014
Text copyright © 2001 by Gloria Jean Pinkney
Illustrations copyright © 2001 by
Jerry Pinkney, Brian Pinkney, and Myles C. Pinkney
All rights reserved
Designed by Atha Tehon
Text set in Centaur
Printed in the U.S.A. on acid-free paper
1 3 5 7 9 10 8 6 4 2
Library of Congress Cataloging-in-Publication Data
Pinkney, Gloria Jean.
In the forest of your remembrance: thirty-three goodly news
tellings for the whole family/Gloria Jean Pinkney;
illustrations by Jerry Pinkney, Brian Pinkney, and Myles C. Pinkney.
p.   cm.
Includes bibliographical references.
ISBN 0-8037-2643-0
1. Pinkney, Gloria Jean. 2. Christian spiritual
biography—United States. 3. Miracles. I. Pinkney, Jerry.
II. Pinkney, J. Brian. III. Pinkney, Myles C. IV. Title.
BR1725.P553 A3 2001
277.3'0825'092—dc21
[B] 00-064488

DEDICATED TO
Ellen Geraldine Ballard (my first prayer partner) and Felicia Bunch
(a prayer partner who told me about the New Jerusalem).
Myrtle Tisdale (ordained prayer warrior and friend),
Minister Linda Councill (a prayer partner and faithful listener),
and Minister Sandra Baker (an excellent educator).
John Olson and Joseph Grazado (MA Turnpike helpers).
Also, my cherished helpmate Jerry Pinkney, our entire family,
and all the people of God.

With heartfelt gratitude
I wish to thank the following teachers for sharing their spiritual gifts
from our Lord Jesus Christ: Reverend Louis V. Jernigan,
Reverend Arthur L. Lewter, Reverend Myrtle Smith,
and the ministerial staff of The Star of Bethlehem Missionary
Baptist Church, Ossining, New York. I also wish to thank
Reverend David Powers of the Briarcliff Congregational Church,
Briarcliff, New York; Evangelist Sherri Bentley; and the media
ministries of evangelist Benny Hinn and
Reverend Charles Stanley. Many thanks also to
Bishop Roderick Caesar of the Full Gospel Tabernacle,
Jamaica Queens, New York, who prayed for me
and taught me to pray for a double portion of spirit.

Contents

THE CREATOR

REFLECTIONS

BIBLE SOURCES

KJV • King James Version (Thomas Nelson, Inc.)

NIV • New International Version (Zondervan Publishing House)

NJB • New Jerusalem Bible (Doubleday)

NKJV • New King James Version (Thomas Nelson, Inc.)

NLT • New Living Translation (Tyndale House Publishers, Inc.)

NRSV • New Revised Standard Version (Thomas Nelson, Inc.)

NWT • New World Translation (Watchtower Bible and Tract Society of New York, Inc. and the International Bible Students Association)

TAB • The Amplified Bible (Zondervan Publishing House)

TAN • Tanakh (The Jewish Publication Society)

TEV • Today's English Version (Thomas Nelson, Inc.)

TLB • The Living Bible (Tyndale House Publishers, Inc.)

The Koran (Penguin Books USA Inc.)

Foreword
Clifton L. Taulbert

In Gloria Jean Pinkney's *In the Forest of Your Remembrance*, we are invited to deeply listen and carefully observe as we share her precious moments of "faith and life." Thank you, Gloria, for reminding us that within the busy structure of our days, there are those ever-present moments when deep listening causes us to carefully observe what we may have overlooked as not important. In your thirty-three remembrances, you remind us of the fellowship of faith and life. Life we readily embrace, but "faith" must somehow prove itself over and over again. Every time I turned a page, faith and life were shown to me as twins. And what a wonderful metaphor for the twins—the Forest, a place that demands quietness and careful observation, less we miss the small things that nature has provided to enhance the life and the look of the giant trees we so readily see. Through the years your work has kept us connected with life, now in these, your honest and personal remembrances, we share with you the source of your life.

Your great-grandfather Reverend N. O. Thompson's pastoral voice, gentle and commanding, comes through your work as you give us permission to become your dear hearers. With such an invitation, we have little choice but to recognize, as did you, that in the Forest of our Remembrance, we are both the prayer and the answer. You have lifted incidental and happenstance to a very high level. From now on I will refer to those events as the results of "deep listening" and "careful observation."

As I read through your manuscript, I could not help but think that the tapestry of human living is woven in ways we may not have anticipated. Is there a story in a blown-out tire? If one does not listen and observe, the story may go undetected. But you listened, and shared with us your thoughts and connected relationships and incidents in ways we may have not. What good is an eraser in a coat pocket? Well, it's of no value unless you really need one and there it is. You needed an eraser and your pencil had none, but you remembered. We all remember, but seldom do we credit a source bigger than ourselves for having done so. Again, the Forest is beautiful, not just because of the big trees, but because we choose to pay attention to the small ground coverings. Maybe you are telling us that there are no small favors, only life impacted by faith.

What do we do or say when things just happen to turn out right? Why hold on to a big rubber band? Well, you have convinced us that it was the right thing for Jerry, your husband, to do. He didn't know this, but his actions would become your answer later on. This book will help many to personalize and anticipate the joy of unselfish living. Now you will have me and others not demoting ourselves, but elevating the role of the twins faith and life. Your personal journey shared will give us cause to stop and think about the unexplained and the coincidences as we go through our lives.

You have chosen to cast nothing aside. You have chosen to value all the life within your Forest, daily growing from your daily living with others. Many of us will embrace your discovery. Some of us may choose to ignore such connections of daily living to deep listening and careful observation. But for all of us, you have provided a daily look at your God.

As we read, embrace, and understand the life-changing impact of these thirty-three personal remembrances of yours, we will be challenged to become dear hearers within our own daily lives and make from your Forest of Remembrance, one of our own.

A Writer's Prayer

PSALM 1:1–3 (KJV) *Blessed is the man that walketh not in the counsel of the ungodly, nor standeth in the way of sinners, nor sitteth in the seat of the scornful. But his delight is in the law of the LORD; and in his law doth he meditate day and night. And he shall be like a tree planted by the rivers of water, that bringeth forth his fruit in his season; his leaf also shall not wither; and whatsoever he doeth shall prosper.*

Abba Father
please lead
and guide
through Your
Holy Spirit
so that I
will realize
when I cease
telling truths
and begin
to create
a new story.
In the
name of
Christ Jesus
I pray… Amen. Amen. Amen.

JOHN 8:31–32 (NLT) *Jesus said to the people who believed in him, "You are truly my disciples if you keep obeying my teachings. And you will know the truth, and the truth will set you free."*

ARISE

Arise, shine,
for your light has dawned;
The Presence of the Lord
has shown upon you!
Behold! Darkness shall cover the earth,
And thick clouds the peoples;
But upon you the Lord will shine,
And His Presence be seen over you.
And nations shall walk by your light,
Kings, by your shining radiance.

ISAIAH 60:1–3
(TAN)

Dayspring in the Dark

LUKE 1:78–79 (NKJV) *Through the tender mercy of our God, With which the Dayspring from on high has visited us; To give light to those who sit in darkness and the shadow of death, To guide our feet into the way of peace.*

It was 1970, the year our family moved from Boston to New York. We had planned to purchase an old Victorian house in Westchester County, but after losing the buyers of our Boston home, we were financially unable to make a purchase in New York. Therefore, we rented the Westchester house with an option to buy. Not long afterward, our vacated house in Boston was vandalized. So Jerry moved back to await a new buyer, while the children and I set up housekeeping in New York.

However, after weeks of struggling with a faulty hot-water heater, insects, a bat, and other rodents in the house, I decided to pack up our station wagon and go stay with Jerry for a while. Our ten-year-old daughter, Troy, was beside me. In back Brian, age nine, Scott, age eight, and Myles, age seven, were sitting atop two mattresses, along with blankets, pillows, toys, and household items. Then, in a hurry, I headed for the Massachusetts Turnpike.

Suddenly, not far from Boston, our left rear tire blew while I was in the passing lane. "Oh, God! Oh, God!" I cried, fruitlessly pressing the brake. Yet our car seemed to be picking up speed. "Oh, Lord," I called, wondering why my voice and those of my kids sounded distant. Again I called to our God as the vehicle fishtailed. Unbeknown to me, grass was wrapping around the deflating tire. Once that wheel could no longer turn, our vehicle turned onto its left side, slid across the highway with sparks flying, abruptly flipped upside down, then finally came to rest in the right lane.

Troy and I found ourselves dangling from the ceiling by safety belts. "Oh, God!" I cried, struggling to free myself, then our daughter. Once loosened, she and I eased through a hole in the windshield. After settling Troy on the roadside, I hurried to open the back hatch. But the door wasn't working. Not a sound was coming from inside, and sparks were flickering near the gas tank. "Oh, God," I called again and again.

Suddenly a car pulled up. Then two men got out. One was carrying a fire extinguisher. "Are you all right, lady?" he asked, taking care of the sparks.

"My boys are inside," I cried. "The latch is stuck." Please Lord, I prayed as the second man repeatedly tried the handle. Finally it worked. "Thank you!" I exclaimed. Promptly the two men pulled out one mattress, then a second.

Suddenly Brian appeared, followed by Scott. "Wow, Mom," Brian said excitedly, "that was great!"

"Did you see us?" asked Scott. "We were all over the road!" Lastly Myles got out with a grin.

Right about then a state trooper came. Meanwhile, the two men drove away before I could thank them again. "You're lucky," the officer said gently as he drove us to his barracks. Then two officers entertained the kids while I telephoned Jerry.

The next day Jerry had an appointment in Boston at an architect's office. During that meeting he happened to mention our accident. "Was your wife driving a station wagon?" asked a man who was employed there. In amazement, Jerry answered yes.

"Did she have four kids with her?" a second employee said, then added, "Were there sparks coming from around her gas tank?" Again my stunned husband said yes. "We stopped, put out the fire, and got your kids out," said the man. Then, in complete astonishment, Jerry thanked them.

At home when Jerry told me about the encounter with our helpers, it had not yet been revealed to us that signs, wonders, and miracles demonstrate the power of our God. Only our Creator knew that a day would come when I would share this telling in a book of remembrance.

I CORINTHIANS 13:11 (NKJV) *When I was a child, I spoke as a child, I understood as a child, I thought as a child; but when I became a man, I put away childish things.*

Jesus Is the Rock

2 SAMUEL 22:32 (NKJV) *For who is God, except the LORD? And who is a rock, except our God?*

Denver, Colorado, is a beautiful city to visit. One year Jerry and I were invited there for book signings. On a bright morning, author Mildred Pitts Walter took us to see one of Denver's highlights: their botanical gardens. We found it to be a plush green paradise surrounded that winter by snow-capped mountains.

As we were leaving, my attention was drawn to a large rock stationed beside an exit door. Upon it there lay a brand-new pencil eraser. *It's for you*, came a still, small thought. So I put it inside my coat pocket.

Later that day Jerry and I had our first signing at a local bookstore. Afterward, as is our custom, we began to browse. Jerry is always looking for reference books. I headed for the journal section. For a while I looked without success. Yet I felt that something special was waiting on the shelves. Finally a russet-colored binding caught my eye. *Season of Renewal*, I read, subtitled, *A Diary for Women Moving Beyond the Loss of a Love*. "Thank you, Lord," I whispered. For a very long time I had been having difficulties writing about my mother's death. *Maybe this diary will help me*, I thought.

"Where did you get this book?" the owner asked at the checkout counter. "Is there another?" I led her to the journal section where I had happened upon it, but there wasn't a second copy. "I recently lost my husband," she told me. "I don't recall ever seeing this book." Right then I offered the diary. "No, no!" she said, refusing to accept. "I'll just order more," she told me. Then, after sharing her sorrow, and explaining why the book was to me a precious discovery, I went back to the register.

It is a habit of mine to write during the night whether at home or on the road. So with pen and journal I crept past Jerry into the hotel bathroom that evening. But as soon as I opened my new diary, a still, small thought came: Your words should be written in pencil. So I tiptoed back into the bedroom, got one out of the desk, and went back.

Then, within moments of beginning to write, I needed to make a correction. "Oh, no!" I said softly, frowning at my writing tool. "An eraserless pencil. Now what am I going to do?" All of a sudden a recollection came. There's an eraser in my jacket pocket, I thought. "Thank you, Lord God!" I whispered.

PSALM 32:8 (NIV) *I will instruct you and teach you in the way you should go; I will counsel you and watch over you.*

He's Alive!

HOSEA 2:18 (KJV) *And in that day will I make a covenant for them with the beasts of the field and with the fowls of heaven, and with the creeping things of the ground: and I will break the bow and the sword and the battle out of the earth, and will make them to lie down safely.*

I was booked on an early flight to New York from Eufaula, Alabama. It was one hour before the flight was scheduled to take off. Yet Eufaula's waiting room was empty. At least that's what I thought until spotting a very, very large caterpillar making its way along the ridges of the tiled floor. We were going in the same direction.

"Incredible," I said under my breath. "I didn't know caterpillars could grow that big." Watching it crawl caused me to feel uneasy. So I took a seat with plenty of space between me and the creature, then began reading.

A short time later I noticed out of the corner of my eye that the caterpillar had taken a turn in the tiles, and was heading my way. This, I thought, is getting creepier and creepier. So I changed my seat.

Moments later the automatic doors opened. In came a man and woman with two children, a boy who appeared to be about three and a girl who looked a few years older. Right away the little boy spotted our fuzzy visitor.

"Look, Mommy," the child yelled. His voice bounced about the empty room. "It's alive!" he said happily. Then the two children began playing a game of losing and finding the caterpillar.

Oh, Lord, I thought. Please don't let them hurt it! However, I didn't have to worry. Both of them were fascinated with their new friend. Long after the girl became bored with their game, the little boy continued to play. Each time he spotted the caterpillar, it was for him a miraculous discovery. "It's alive," the youngster called over and over again.

I continued reading the Scriptures. That creature has the breath of life, just as we have, I thought. Suddenly our risen Savior came to mind. Christ Jesus is alive too! I thought.

Now, a few months later our family took its annual visit to Cape Cod National Seashore. On the last day of another summer vacation, our next-door neighbor Ellie stopped by.

"Look what I found on my tomato plant," she said. To our amazement there was a very large, long bright-green chrysalis attached to her plant. It was just beginning to open. Within it we saw a silky cocoon, soon to become one of God's flying creatures. Immediately I remembered the Eufaula airport caterpillar. How wonderful it is, I thought, to experience a new birth!

JOHN 3:3 (TAB) *Jesus answered him, I assure you, most solemnly I tell you, that unless a person is born again (anew, from above), he cannot ever see (know, be acquainted with, and experience) the kingdom of God.*

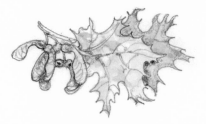

Look What I Have Here for You

ROMANS 8:27–28 (NKJV) *Now He who searches the hearts knows what the mind of the Spirit is, because He makes intercession for the saints according to the will of God. And we know that all things work together for good to those who love God, to those who are the called according to His purpose.*

It was the Sunday before Mother's Day 1998. I was seated beside a little girl and her mother at The Star of Bethlehem Missionary Baptist Church. It had been an exceptionally long evening service, and the mother had become concerned when the child could no longer keep still. I happened to have a writing tablet, so I offered them paper and pencil. After church the child presented me with a drawing. "Please sign it," I said. *From Jasmine*, she wrote, thanked me, then waved good-bye.

The following Sunday morning, as I was rushing to arrive early for The Star Mother's Day Breakfast, I came to an abrupt stop when a still, small thought came to mind. Take Jasmine one of your books, said our Lord. Promptly I signed a copy of *The Sunday Outing*. After slipping it into a gift bag, I hurried off to church.

Our Mother's Day Breakfast was an inspiring program. Uplifting to all present was the moment when a little girl began singing "He Is So Wonderful." Instantly the Holy Spirit filled the room. This song is lengthy, yet the young soloist sang steadfastly even though tears were streaming down her face. When she finished, the congregation gave resounding applause. It had truly been a blessing.

Immediately afterward our 11:00 worship began. However, to my great disappointment, neither Jasmine nor her mother were in attendance. Following service I stayed a while in the sanctuary to greet friends. All of a sudden my attention was drawn toward a back entrance. Our little soloist from the Mother's Day Breakfast was coming down the center aisle. I beckoned to her. "You sang beautifully this morning," I said. She responded with a grin. Then I told her about my fears when as a child I was often called upon to sing solo. "I always sang with a tremor," I confessed, giving an animated demonstration. Her grin grew broader. "Our Lord will always help you," I concluded, then added, "I know your parents well, but have forgotten your name."

"Jasmine," she said shyly. My face broke out into an even bigger smile than hers.

"Jasmine!" I exclaimed, reaching into my bag. "Look what I have here for you!" With a joyful heart I handed the little singer her book. Thank you, Holy Spirit, I silently prayed, for telling me to bring it. Then Jasmine gave me a hug, and walked away with a bounce.

ACTS 2:17 (NLT) *In the last days, God said, I will pour out my Spirit upon all people. Your sons and daughters will prophesy, your young men will see visions, and your old men will dream dreams.*

New York to Chicago

I PETER 1:7 (NKJV) *That the genuineness of your faith, being much more precious than gold that perishes, though it is tested by fire, may be found to praise, honor, and glory at the revelation of Jesus Christ...*

One day while I was on board an airplane with my husband, Jerry, a steward stopped by our seats. "Pardon me," he said, smiling, "what is your name?"

"Gloria Jean Pinkney," I said. "Why do you ask?"

"You strongly resemble my friend Renee," he replied. "She lives in San Francisco. Do you have a sister there?"

"My sisters live in Los Angeles," I explained.

Later I was studying an electronic Bible (the King James Version) when the steward came by to serve refreshments. "What are you reading?" he asked with a curious expression on his face.

I smiled back, then held it up for him to see. It was I Samuel 3:10. "And the Lord came, and stood, and called as at other times, 'Samuel, Samuel!' Then Samuel answered, 'Speak, for thy servant heareth.'"

The steward's face lit up. "I gave an electronic Bible to my niece," he said excitedly. Then he added, "Maybe it's time for me to buy one for myself." Thank you, Lord, I thought, for allowing me to strengthen one of your believers.

Just before we exited the flight, I discovered a small piece of paper inside my coat pocket. It was the daily word from a desk calendar. Should I give it to him? I inquired of the Lord. Instantly I felt his approval.

However, the steward was nowhere in sight. Lord, I wondered, did I misunderstand? Well, when we reached the waiting room, I spotted him. So with a pleased smile I handed over the Scripture. It was also from the book of Samuel, 2 Samuel 7:3—"And Nathan said to the king, 'Go, do all that is in thine heart, for the Lord is with thee.'" The steward thanked me, then Jerry and I headed on our way.

Ten minutes later, after making a few stops, we happened upon him once again. "How did you know that I was a Christian?" he asked with a puzzled expression on his face.

"I could tell," was my answer. The steward looked pleased. Later, after he had gone, I prayed this prayer: Forgive me, Lord. I should have said, "The Holy Spirit revealed you to me, and me to you."

GALATIANS 6:9–10 (NKJV) *And let us not grow weary while doing good, for in due season we shall reap if we do not lose heart. Therefore, as we have opportunity, let us do good to all, especially to those who are of the household of faith.*

Myrtle Tree

LUKE 7:22 (NKJV) *Jesus answered and said to them, "Go and tell John the things you have seen and heard: that the blind see, the lame walk, the lepers are cleansed, the deaf hear, the dead are raised, the poor have the gospel preached to them."*

There was a lovely woman watching me. I felt her eyes as I sat in LaGuardia Airport thinking about a Sunday school lesson that had been taught that morning by Reverend Myrtle Smith at The Star of Bethlehem Missionary Baptist Church. Unfortunately it had been necessary for me to leave early because of an author visit in Winston-Salem, North Carolina.

Suddenly the woman got up, then sat two seats away. "Excuse me," she said in a genteel voice. "My name is Myrtle Tisdale. We don't know each other, but I believe the Lord has led me to speak with you." Right away a good feeling came over me. Here was another twin occurrence, Myrtle and Myrtle. Listen, said his still, small voice. I smiled back, then introduced myself while admiring her silver-gray curls, bright eyes, and glowing skin. "I'm an ordained prayer warrior," she told me. I couldn't help grinning. Thank you, Lord, I thought as my new acquaintance talked about ministering to the sick.

"I'm a prayer warrior also," I said afterward. Then I talked about an incident that had occurred a few months earlier while I was attending a spiritual retreat. "Sister Gloria," Minister Wanda Faye Myers had called to me as I was preparing to leave. "The Lord told me to tell you something." What could it be, I wondered as the minister approached me with a radiant smile. "You're a prayer warrior!" she announced. Myrtle's eyes grew brighter.

"Her words were a confirmation," I told Myrtle. "Only our Lord knew that at his bidding I had been encouraging people to say as well as write their daily prayers. I had never heard of a prayer warrior until that day at the retreat," I said. "Now the Lord has sent me one who is ordained!" Right then we exchanged telephone numbers and promised to pray for each other. Too soon it was time to board.

Not long afterward Myrtle and I adopted each other as sisters in Christ, and I began calling her Myrtle Tree, a name fitting for one so grounded in faith. One day while she and her daughter-in-love, Linda Faye, visited my home in New York, our Lord gave another startling confirmation when I overheard Linda Faye address Myrtle as Sugar. "Everybody calls her Sugar," Linda Faye told me. My mouth fell open. Thank you, Lord, I thought. Then I told them about my prayer partner Fay Sugar, who is called Sugar Fay at the care center where she resides.

More than a year later our Lord revealed a greater purpose in bringing Myrtle Tree and me together. "Gloria," said my cousin Marilyn, "I need to have a kidney removed. But I'm not certain that I should." Marilyn was calling me from Atlanta. That day the usual soft tones in her southern way of speaking were barely audible. "I need your prayers," she said softly. Right then we prayed to our Lord for an answer. All of a sudden I heard his still, small voice: Call Myrtle.

"My friend Myrtle is an ordained prayer warrior, Marilyn,"

I announced. "Her prayers are Spirit-filled. I'll ask her to call you." Afterward I telephoned Myrtle Tree and as always she responded with *Yes!*

"Gloria," Marilyn said excitedly when she called back, "did you know that your friend Myrtle has one kidney?"

"No," I said, feeling an ever-deepening love for our Creator God. However, after Marilyn's successful surgery I was able to recall that when I first met Myrtle Tree, she had told me about her operation that had taken place twenty years before our paths crossed.

EPHESIANS 3:17–19 (KJV) *That Christ may dwell in your hearts by faith; that ye, being rooted and grounded in love, May be able to comprehend with all saints what is the breadth, and length, and depth, and height; And to know the love of Christ, which passeth knowledge, that ye might be filled with all the fulness of God.*

Never a Time
When She Couldn't Pray

2 TIMOTHY 1:3 (NKJV) *I thank God, whom I serve with a pure conscience, as my forefathers did, as without ceasing I remember you in my prayers night and day.*

"Aunt Naomi," I said after we had been sharing Scriptures, singing favorite hymns, and praying, "has there ever been a time in your life when you couldn't pray?" Aunt Roxie Naomi Thompson, although critically ill, still maintained a soft-spoken, yet sometimes fiery way of expressing her faith.

She raised herself up in the bed, supported by an alarmingly frail-looking arm. "There wasn't never a time when I couldn't pray," exclaimed my eighty-seven-year-old aunt. "It's all you need." My cousin Dorisenia was also by her side that day. She and I reaped the benefits from a perpetual prayer's personal testimony. When I returned home, I learned more about the importance of prayer.

"Lord," I said one morning while meditating in bed, "how may I help myself and others to pray more?" Right then a crystal clear thought came: Pray by day of birth. "What a good idea," I responded. "Thank you."

At breakfast I explained the prayer plan given. "Whenever I see your birth number," I told Jerry, "a prayer goes up for you."

Then I began to worry. Lord, I prayed, there are family, friends, and prayer partners to remember. That's a lot of numbers. Please help!

Soon an awesome confirmation came with signals to prove the importance of continuous prayer. I was driving home from the dentist's office when a car turned in front of me with our oldest grandchild's birthday number on its license plate. Immediately I prayed for Gloria Nicole. Within moments another vehicle slipped in behind the first. It also had those same two numbers. So I said a second prayer. When it occurred a third time, an uneasy feeling swept over me. "Lord," I said after praying, "you're telling me that something is wrong." Promptly I turned toward Gloria's school.

Gloria Nicole wasn't at the after-school program or the library. Then I headed toward her street. "Mom-Mom," she called excitedly when I saw her waving to me. We were just a few blocks from her home. "I prayed you would come. Did Granddaddy tell you?" she asked, getting into my car. I shook my head, feeling in awe of God. "You know Mommy doesn't want me in our apartment building alone. Granddaddy had an appointment. He told me to walk slowly. He said you were expected soon, and he'd leave you a note." Finally Gloria Nicole paused to take a deep breath. "If Granddaddy didn't tell you," she said, "how did you know?"

"Glory," I responded, using her nickname, "the Holy Spirit told me!" Her eyes grew wider than usual. "Remember what I told you about birthdays and prayer?" She nodded. Then I told her about the Lord's signposts. "From now on, Glory," I added, "whenever we see the birth dates of family, friends, or prayer partners," I said, "it's time to pray for them." Later it was revealed to me to use Gloria's birth date to pray for all (eight up to now) of our grandchildren.

Now, my dear readers, this gift from our Lord will increase

fellowship with Him. Regrettably, I shared this blessing with a prayer partner who, after having birth numbers revealed in a dream, used them to gamble. "Look what the Lord did," my friend said excitedly after gambling and winning $750.

Right away I realized that a lesson was being given from our Lord. Forgive me, Lord Jesus, I prayed when she told me, for causing a friend to stumble. I neglected to tell her that Godly gifts are for Godly things. "It wasn't our Lord's doing," I told my friend, "it came from the destroyer."

ROMANS 12:2 (NIV) *Do not conform any longer to the pattern of this world, but be transformed by the renewing of your mind. Then you will be able to test and approve what God's will is—his good, pleasing and perfect will.*

Lord, Help!

JEREMIAH 33:2–3 (KJV) *Thus saith the LORD the maker thereof, the LORD that formed it, to establish it; the LORD is his name; Call unto me, and I will answer thee, and shew thee great and mighty things, which thou knowest not.*

"I heard a good joke," my husband, Jerry, said as he came into the kitchen. "But you may not like it," he added. "It's a religious one."

"I don't want to hear it," I responded, then went into the laundry room. Right away a still, small thought came. Listen.... There is something for you to learn. "I've changed my mind," I called out.

Jerry had a pleased expression on his face when I came back. "There was a man who wanted to win the lottery," he began. I raised an eyebrow, but held my tongue. "Over and over again the man prayed," he said, "but without success. Then the man had an idea. 'God,' he cried out, 'if you let me win, I'll only keep a small amount for myself, and give the rest away!' Afterward, the man went to bed." I waited patiently for the punch line.

"Late that night," said Jerry, "God woke the man up. 'Help me out here,' God said. 'Buy yourself a ticket!' Isn't that funny?" Jerry said, laughing. I gave him a little smile, then went on with what I had been doing.

Right away another still, small thought came. "There is a lesson in that joke for me," I called out. "If I want to have a third book published, I'll have to work harder. The Lord won't write it for me!"

A few weeks later a second valuable lesson came. Jerry and I were attending an American Library Association convention in San Francisco. After one day of walking up and down steep hills in wedge-heeled shoes, I had a foot breakdown. Lord, I prayed after soaking my feet in hot water, please make them stop hurting! Then I went to bed. Late that night another thought came from our Lord: Help me out here. Buy sensible shoes!

The next morning off I went toward Macy's department store. Turn around. Go the other way, came his still, small voice. Immediately I headed in the opposite direction, crossed at the corner, turned left, then walked up a hill. To my surprise, I spotted a store with Easy Spirit shoes. "Thank you, Jesus, for answering my prayer," I said, attending the rest of the ALA functions in sensible, comfortable flats.

PROVERBS 2:10 (NLT) *For wisdom will enter your heart, and knowledge will fill you with joy.*

Enter, Rest, and Pray

PSALM 77:13 (KJV) *Thy way, O God, is in the sanctuary: who is so great a God as our God?*

"I wish you could be here for that interview, Mom," said Troy Bernardette. We had been discussing an upcoming meeting with Mrs. Muccigrosso, the principal of Saint Ann's Parish School in Ossining, New York. Although we are Protestant, our family agreed after my author visit there that an education based on religious principals would be best for Gloria Nicole's middle-school years. However, on the day of Troy's meeting I was a visiting author at Saint Joseph's Catholic School in Cincinnati, Ohio.

"Our program is not in the school building today," said my escort when we arrived at Saint Joseph's School. "You're speaking in our chapel." So, putting all concerns away about not being home for our daughter, I spoke wholeheartedly on the subject of "Writing From Life Experiences." Lord, I thought, speaking from the pulpit to so many well-behaved, listening children, it's good to be in such a place.

Afterward, as I sat waiting in a car, I looked up at their lovely old edifice. In awe I read the words engraved above the door of Saint Ann's Chapel.

Enter, Rest, and Pray.

"Guess what, Mom," Troy Bernardette said excitedly when

later that evening I responded to the blinking light on my hotel telephone.

"Gloria's going to Saint Ann's," I responded. Of course our daughter couldn't figure out how I knew. "The Holy Spirit showed me," I said, then told her about my day.

ACTS 2:39 (TAB) *For the promise (of the Holy Spirit) is to and for you and your children, and to and for all that are far away, (even) to and for as many as the Lord our God invites and bids to come to Himself.*

Color of Hope

ROMANS 5:5 (NKJV) *Now hope does not disappoint, because the love of God has been poured out in our hearts by the Holy Spirit who was given to us.*

Yellow is a color of hope, said his still, small voice early one morning. When winter ends, the earth opens. Which flowers are brightest? I lay in bed thinking about what I had heard from the Lord. Instantly daffodils, forsythia, and dandelions came to mind. Much later when researching yellow blooms in an encyclopedia, I found cloth-of-gold crocus, sunflowers, and many other light-giving plants.

That morning at breakfast I shared my awakening with Jerry. Soon, as with other gifts, a confirmation came. We were scheduled to speak at an Iowa teachers' conference. On the way to LaGuardia Airport, as we exited onto a service road, our front left tire blew. "This is a dangerous place to be," said Jerry with an anxious tone in his voice. "Call 911." Large and small vehicles were maneuvering around us at alarming speeds. Immediately I took out our cellular phone.

After giving our location to an operator, I prayed. Instantly I felt clearheaded. "We've forgotten about triple A!" I said, then called our automobile club. Our dilemma had blocked our thinking. Wisely, Jerry always insists that we allow extra time before flights in case of delays. Nevertheless, it appeared, after waiting a while, that we were going to miss our plane. "Maybe you can direct traffic while I change the tire," Jerry said with an unsure look on his face. Yet his hand was on the door handle. Oh, God! I thought.

Right then a bright-yellow tow truck arrived. "Yes," I said excitedly. "Yellow is a color of hope. Thank you, Lord!" I exclaimed. Jerry beamed.

However, the driver got out of the truck shaking his head. "Sorry, folks," the man said. He had come in response to the AAA call. "I can't help you here. I'll get myself killed." Jerry's smile froze. Help us, Lord, I prayed. Within seconds another bright-yellow tow truck pulled up in back of our car. He had come in response to the 911 call. "Maybe I can get him to cover me while I change your flat," the first driver told us. Both trucks belonged to Jamaica Towing. The two men did not openly appear to be acquainted, but the second driver was willing. He remained in his truck (which was deterring traffic) while the man from AAA changed our tire. I couldn't stop grinning as we rode to the airport, realizing that I had just been gifted with another telling. Thank you, Lord God, I prayed when we got to our departing gate just in time to board. "Yellow is a color of hope," I said happily.

What a perfectly clear day, I thought on our flights from New York to Chicago, and then Chicago to Iowa. The earth was glistening with sunshine. As usual, my face was pressed up against a window. Jerry was in the middle seat.

Suddenly I became aware of small and larger patches of golden yellow upon the ground beneath us as we traveled from state to state. "School-bus yards," I said excitedly. "Golden yellow vehicles

transporting hope for tomorrow," I told Jerry, "...our children."
Thank you, Lord, I prayed silently, for opening our eyes to
a color of hope.

"As plain as the nose on your face," my great-aunt Alma
would often say when I couldn't find some item that she had sent
me for. Great-Aunt's distinct way of communicating became a
writing voice for me. It is heard in *Back Home*, my first book for
children, and its prequel, *The Sunday Outing*, my second. "If it was
a snake, it woulda bit you" was another one of Great-Aunt's say-
ings from her growing-up years on a farm. I had not yet been
graced with, as it is described in the Bible, eyes that see and ears
that hear.

Thank God I am now able—through his Holy Spirit—to see
more clearly. Yet, so many of his signposts still go undetected. For
instance, my mother, Ernestine, was a seamstress. She worked in a
children's clothing factory. The last dress that she brought home
to me was a brilliant yellow. It is a favorite color. I feel certain
that it was my mother's also. For when she died suddenly at the
age of twenty-seven, I was given three of her possessions: one was
a yellow suit, which I wore when playing dress up.

Yellow is an important element in my husband's illustrations.
He uses it to bring light and focus to a subject. In *Back Home*,
Ernestine, my eight-year-old heroine, wears a bright-yellow
pinafore.

About four years ago (before the yellow tellings), at the
prompting of our three oldest grandchildren—Leon, Charnelle,
and Gloria Nicole—we turned an old storage shed into a writing
place for me. It sits in a wooded area. The surrounding grounds
are occupied by wildlife.

It all happened one day when Leon overheard me complaining
about not having a quiet place to work. "Grandma," he said, "you
know that old shack out back?" I nodded. "We're going to fix it

up for you," he said excitedly. Then they ran off. That will keep them occupied for a while, I thought. Little did I know that an answer to my problem was just a hundred feet from our home. "Come and see," our grandchildren called later that afternoon. As I stepped through the debris that they had taken out, hope blossomed within me.

"Why, it's perfect!" I said. Before me was a 14' x 14' wooden structure with beveled windows. It had been built as a playhouse by the former owners of our home. For more than twenty years we had been using it for storage. Leon, Charnelle, and Gloria Nicole beamed. Once dry walls, electricity, and heat were added, I moved in. "We're going to call it Sunflower," I announced. You see, just a short time earlier I had become attracted to sunflower collectibles. Thank you, Lord, I prayed. Our God had given me hope, a place in which I would write about him, and the gift was given through our grandchildren.

EPHESIANS 1:3 (TLB) *How we praise God, the Father of our Lord Jesus Christ, who has blessed us with every blessing in heaven because we belong to Christ.*

Hinds' Feet on High Places

HEBREWS 2:4 (NLT) *And God verified the message by signs and wonders and various miracles and by giving gifts of the Holy Spirit whenever he chose to do so.*

"Take up your swords," a Fall revivalist told the congregation. I was attending a service at my third home church, The Star of Bethlehem Missionary Baptist Church in Ossining, New York. Immediately I responded by opening my Holy Bible. My King James Version revealed Psalm 18. Then I waited for further instructions. "Psalm eighteen, verses thirty-two to thirty-three," said our spiritual leader. I stared at God's word in wonder. The Holy Spirit had led me to the right page.

My friend Willa was standing beside me that incredible night. She and I stared in amazement at the Scripture that had been readied for reading. Willa raised her eyebrows with a questioning expression on her face. "It's the Lord," I whispered. Her face glowed with an understanding smile. Then we read Psalm 18:32–33 in unison. "It is God that girdeth me with strength, And maketh my way perfect. He maketh my feet like hinds' feet, And setteth me upon my high places."

A few weeks later, in an airport bookstore, I began searching for something inspirational. Then, while spinning a rack, I spotted a paperback with deer on its jacket cover. For you, came a powerfully strong thought. I read the title, *Hinds' Feet on High Places,* by Hannah Hurnard. So I looked inside, and read Psalm 18:33, then Habakkuk 3:19, as a blessed feeling swept over me. "Thank you, Lord," I prayed.

Later I learned that a similar Scripture is found in 2 Samuel 22:32–34, but for some reason I favored Habakkuk 3:19 over the others. Then one day I realized why. Our wedding anniversary is March 19.

PSALM 19:1 (KJV) *The heavens declare the glory of God; and the firmament sheweth his handywork.*

BELIEVE

If I do not the works of my Father,
believe me not.
But if I do,
though ye believe not me,
believe the works:
that ye may know,
and believe,
that the Father *is* in me,
and I in him.

JOHN 10:37–38
(KJV)

Good Hair Days

PSALM 128:1 (NKJV) *Blessed is every one who fears the LORD, Who walks in His ways.*

I love to sing. On June 10, 1995, I was in our kitchen preparing to dye my hair while softly singing a tune from the movie *South Pacific*. I changed a few words to suit my reason for being up early. "I'm going to wash that gray right out of my hair," I sang while opening a box of light golden brown dye. "I'm going to wash that gray right out of my hair," I sang while arranging towels. "I'm going to wash that gray right out of my hair," I sang with gusto when testing the tap water. "And send it on its way!"

Suddenly a message from the Holy Spirit came: You haven't read your Scriptures today.

"Oh, I haven't read my Scriptures today," I repeated. So I headed for my devotional window. After saying a prayer, I opened my *One Year Bible*, which is 365 daily readings taken from the New King James Version. It was given to me by my first prayer partner, Ellen Geraldine Ballard. As always the text began with an Old Testament reading, followed by the New, then a psalm, and lastly some verses from Proverbs. "Oh, my God!" I said after reading Proverbs 16:31. "Lord," I asked, "are you telling me not to dye my hair? But, Lord," I said, "I'm going to look so much older."

"The silver-haired head is a crown of glory," I read, "If it is found in the way of righteousness." Then I went to check some other translations. "White hair is a crown of glory and is seen most among the godly," said The Living Bible. Oh, dear, I thought, then opened my New World Translation of the Holy Scriptures. "Gray-headedness is a crown of beauty when it is found in the way of righteousness." Lastly I got my King James Version. "The hoary head is a crown of glory, if it be found in the way of righteousness." "Yes, Lord," I said in surrender, "gray hair it is for Gloria!"

ROMANS 11:33 (KJV) *O the depth of the riches both of the wisdom and knowledge of God! how unsearchable are his judgments, and his ways past finding out!*

Apple of His Eye

I KINGS 19:7 (NRSV) *The angel of the LORD came a second time, touched him, and said, "Get up and eat, otherwise the journey will be too much for you."*

"Keep me as the apple of Your eye; Hide me under the shadow of Your wings" (Psalm 17:8 NKJV) has for a long while been a favored Scripture. I came to realize why after awaking one morning in a troubled state of mind. Instead of stopping for breakfast, I grabbed a rosy red apple that had been given to me during a school visit. Then I headed for Sunflower, my writing shed behind our home.

Upon entering I knelt in prayer before my tiny meditation window. "Lord," I called, "why wasn't 'Jesse's Cloud' accepted?" I had submitted a fictional story based on my great-great-grand-father's and great-grandfather's circuit ministries in North Carolina. I had written the story in rhyme. However, my publisher felt that it needed to be rewritten in prose.

"Lord," I said, "I know that you gave me this idea. I've been given such positive responses to this rhyme from teachers. I don't know what to do. Help me, please!"

Suddenly a comforting sense of well-being swept over me, and I got up feeling enlightened. It's going to be all right, came a clear thought from our Creator God. I felt hungry. So I took a bite out of the apple. Then my attention was drawn to a little book lying among many on a file cabinet. Pick it up, came the word from our Lord. That book was *Small Miracles*. You've been circulating it all around the country, came another thought. Yet, you haven't finished reading it.

Immediately I opened to the bookmark. The story is about a man imprisoned in a Nazi concentration camp when he was a boy. One day a little girl, who was also a prisoner, tossed him a red apple over the barbed wire fence dividing them. My mouth fell open. "Oh, my God!" I exclaimed, staring in awe at the apple that I was holding. "Thank you, Lord," I said joyfully, feeling blessed by our God's love. "It is going to be all right!" Afterward, I went back to what is usually the first reading of my day, the Holy Scriptures.

Then one evening before going to bed I lay reading a new book on the workings of the Holy Spirit. It had been recommended by a salesperson at a local Christian bookstore. After a while I put it away, feeling confused about the gift of tongues. Lord, I prayed before going to bed, I know that I have a personal relationship with you, but I have never spoken in tongues. Afterward, I fell into a restless sleep.

A few hours later I awoke feeling unusually hungry. Jerry was away at the time, so I turned on a lamp and headed for the kitchen. Immediately my eyes focused on a bowl of rosy red apples. I picked one and went back to my bedroom. All at once a very clear thought came to mind: Turn on the television set; there is something for you to see. It was 3:42 A.M., and the dial was tuned to the Public Broadcasting Service.

I nibbled on my apple, watching as a brilliant blue sky appeared with white clouds and one floating red apple. The show was entitled *Newton's Apple*. "Wow," I said. Then I quickly found a pad and made a drawing. Thank you, Lord, I thought. Now I know that I have your Holy Spirit!

Later I recalled the Bible text that we had to memorize in the Holy Spirit Institute class at Star Church, John 16:13 (KJV): "Howbeit when he, the Spirit of truth, is come, he will guide you into all truth: for he shall not speak of himself; but whatsoever he shall hear, that shall he speak; and he will shew you things to come." That is just what happened, I thought. The Holy Spirit had awakened me just in time to see *Newton's Apple*, and had given two confirmations. Both apples were signposts of God's presence and power.

Several months after my "red apple blessing," a telephone call came from a librarian at Mount Pleasant-Blythdale School. It is connected to the Blythedale Children's Hospital in Valhalla, New York. It felt good to be invited for a second time. On both occasions I had found it a special place for learning while healing. I spoke in the hospital cafeteria. Again I had an audience of appreciative and attentive faces. "Would you stay for lunch?" the librarian asked. "Then if you have a few minutes, we'll take you on a tour of our new building and you can meet some of our students."

"Certainly," I replied, although my first thought was that I should go home and write. After eating, we visited their new library. It was a happy space with wonderful book jackets displayed everywhere that I looked. Also, classrooms appeared to be well-equipped, and were decorated with cheerful pictures. "What an inspiring and uplifting place to be," I said.

The science room was our last stop. Upon my entrance, colorful posters, numerous class projects, and hardworking students invited my attention. Later, when turning to leave, I noticed a blue sky scene up on the wall, with white clouds and one floating rosy red apple. My heart skipped a beat. "Where did you get this poster?" I asked.

"A friend just sent it to brighten our room," the science

teacher responded. Then I shared my apple telling. "*Newton's Apple*," he explained afterward, "was aired late at night so that teachers could make tapes to show their students. Here," he said, taking it off of the wall. "It's for you."

"Thank you!" I exclaimed, rolling it up. "This is a third confirmation. It will be added to my memory box (one of many containers in which I keep my Holy Spirit remembrances) to show at presentations." Thanks, Lord, I thought on my way home, for guiding me to linger a little longer.

ACTS 11:16 (TAB) *Then I recalled the declaration of the Lord, How He said, John indeed baptized with water, but you shall be baptized with (be placed in, introduced into) the Holy Spirit.*

The Fish Ain't Bitin'!

JOHN 21:5–6 (NJB) *Jesus called out, "Haven't you caught anything, friends?" And when they answered, "No," he said, "Throw the net out to starboard and you'll find something." So they threw the net out and could not haul it in because of the quantity of fish.*

"Mom," Troy Bernardette said on the telephone, "can you meet Gloria and me at White Plains Hospital? We'd really like to have you with us." Immediately I agreed. Gloria Nicole was scheduled to have an MRI, and was feeling nervous. I had been led to call Troy's house after noticing an issue of *Focus on the Family* magazine. It was on a table near the door at a dialysis center where I had just driven my prayer partner Minister Linda C. for treatment.

After Linda was settled, I went to visit Sugar Fay, another prayer partner who resides in a care center that was close by. There was a short space in time before Gloria Nicole's appointment. However, that day Sugar was exceptionally chatty, so I stayed longer than planned.

"Lord, is this the right place?" I asked when entering the MRI waiting room at White Plains Hospital. The receptionist's booth and the room were empty. The only sign of life was coming from a television screen. Then I noticed a lone jacket lying half-on and half-off of a chair. "Thank you," I said with a sigh of relief. "It's Gloria Nicole's!"

Right at that moment, a nurse came through a swinging door. "Sorry," she told me after I identified myself. "The procedure has already begun. No one is allowed to go in now." Suddenly I had an overwhelming feeling of "all-rightness." So I took a seat and began writing in a notebook. At that time I was working on "Jesse's Tree."

All of a sudden the TV volume got louder. Lord, I thought, there must be something you want me to hear. I looked up just as a news reporter was introducing himself and a fisherman. Then I heard these words: Scott, Carter, and Bryant. Here it is, Lord, I thought. For their names closely resembled those of our sons, Scott, Myles Carter, and Brian. "How's it going?" asked the interviewer.

"The fish ain't bitin'," said the fisherman. Right away I wrote down his response. To me his words were musical, and I suspected because of their names that this occurrence might have a deeper meaning. Thank you, Lord, I thought. I didn't know it, but a new true telling was unfolding, and its title was given beforehand.

A few moments later a woman and a girl who looked to be about seven came in. The child's face looked as if she had suffered much, and she was in a state of anxiety. I couldn't help overhearing as her mother spoke soothing words. Lord, I prayed, tell me if you would have me try to help them. Instantly within me I felt his yes. After introductions I learned that because of the child's fears, she had, after several attempts, been unable to have a much-needed MRI.

"I know a Scripture that will help," I said. "Would you like to hear it?" Both of them nodded. Then I read Jeremiah 17:14 (KJV) from my electronic Bible: "Heal me, O Lord, and I shall be healed; save me, and I shall be saved: for thou art my praise." Jeremiah's prayer for deliverance had been recited to my daughter, when she was ailing, by her husband's mother, Dorothy Lee.

Right then a loud cry came from inside the MRI room. "Mrs. Pinkney," a nurse called, "please come in. Your grand-daughter is trying to get off of the MRI table!"

"Glory," I said, as Troy Bernardette rubbed her forehead caressingly, "there's a very ill little girl in the waiting room. She's afraid of having an MRI. If you cooperate, you can show her how easy it is." Gloria Nicole had become upset after hearing that she was to be injected with a blue liquid. "Look," I said, noticing a familiar symbol upon the butterfly needle in the nurse's hand. "The cross of Jesus is on it. He's here with you right now!" Instantly Gloria Nicole relaxed. Then she accepted the needle prick in silence, and went willingly under the open MRI machine.

At long last it was over. "We memorized that Scripture," the mother told us when we found them in the waiting hall, just out-side the MRI entrance. Then, with smiling faces, they recited in unison.

"Hi!" Gloria Nicole said with a little smile and a wave when she came out. Then she headed straight for the exit. My grand-daughter had done what I had asked her to do, and was eager to leave her ordeal behind.

I left the hospital that day with the images and voices of that mother and child locked in my mind. Thank you, Lord, I prayed, for allowing me to share your Word. Later, while writing this telling, these events brought to mind the healing miracles per-formed by the fishermen who became disciples of our Lord Jesus Christ.

MATTHEW 4:18–19 (NJB) *As he was walking by the Lake of Galilee he saw two brothers, Simon, who was called Peter, and his brother Andrew; they were making a cast into the lake with their net, for they were fishermen. And he said to them, "Come after me and I will make you fishers of people."*

Angela's Kids

JOHN 15:15 (NKJV) *No longer do I call you servants, for a servant does not know what his master is doing; but I have called you friends, for all things that I heard from My Father I have made known to you.*

"This project calls for a boy model about seven," said Jerry one morning at breakfast. He had been invited to work on a special assignment, entitled "For Every Child," in association with UNICEF. As always Jerry gave me a brief description of the child he envisioned for his illustration. I agreed to begin searching, then went out to do Saturday chores.

First stop was at a local shopping center. There, standing beside a burgundy Chevy, was my friend and prayer partner Edith and three of her four grandsons. "I have something to show you," Edith said excitedly, unfolding several news clippings.

"That's me in those pictures with Senator Kennedy," Tevin, youngest of the boys, said proudly. "Me and my mom went to Washington." Tevin, who had been receiving dialysis treatments, had miraculously received a new kidney. He was one of two youngsters chosen by the Kidney Foundation to make a plea before Congress for children in need of transplants.

"He's a miracle," proclaimed Edith. Suddenly I decided to ask Edith if Tevin could model for UNICEF. She informed me that her daughter Angela was in the bank, cashing checks.

"This is perfect," responded Angela as she counted out cash to her older sons, Damian and William. They had recently modeled for a fashion designer, and were happily receiving their earnings. Tevin, however, looked devastated.

"Where's my money?" he said. Promptly I hired Tevin to model for Jerry's illustration for UNICEF. His heart-shaped face perked up, then drooped again. "When?" he asked. I assured him that it would be soon. Well, to everyone's delight, all three ended up posing. Only our Lord knew that another telling was unfolding.

"Got to run," said Angela. "Brandon, my oldest, is in a baseball game." Suddenly a crystal clear message came: Give Angela the prayer journal that is in your car. I obeyed. Both mother and daughter looked pleased.

"See you at Star tomorrow," I said. However, they had plans to attend a Family Day celebration at New Hope Institutional Baptist Church in Tarrytown, New York.

The next morning, as I was heading out to the first of four worship services, word came from our Lord: Take this music to Angela. I had been listening to Valerie Boyd's Scripture-based gospel music as I prepared for Sunday school. But, Lord, I thought, they won't be at Star today. All the same, I put the CD in my purse.

After spending time at Sunday school, I left early to worship with Jerry at Briarcliff Congregational Church for their 10:00 to 11:00 service. Afterward I headed back to Star, hoping to get there before devotionals ended. Boy, that car is in a hurry, I thought when a burgundy Chevy abruptly turned in front of me. Then, to my surprise, four heads became visible through the vehicle's rear window. "Lord," I asked, "is that Edith's car? It is!" I exclaimed. "But how can I catch them?" All of a sudden their automobile pulled over to a curb. So, in astonishment, I parked in front of them as Angela ran into a grocery store.

After explaining our Lord's bidding to Edith, I attempted to leave the CD for Angela with her. I didn't want to be any later than necessary. "Please wait and tell her yourself," responded Edith. "She's just buying a pair of stockings." Lord, I thought later, recalling the look of amazement on Angela's face when I handed her the CD, you're awesome!

Later that day, while attending an evening program at Star, a visiting deacon asked for personal testimonies. Immediately I stood, and spoke about the marvelous gift our God had bestowed earlier upon Angela, her family, and me. "Amen!" the congregation resounded.

Then, near the end of that service, while waiting to approach the offering table, I happened to look toward the rear of Star's sanctuary. There, just a few rows behind me, was Edith, Angela, and her four boys. Damian and Tevin were waving hello. Was the testimony all right, Lord? I wondered, smiling at them. Immediately a feeling of inner peace came as Angela and her mother returned my smile. Thank you, Lord! I prayed.

A few Sundays later Star's congregation stood as Damian and Tevin marched up its aisle toward the altar. Both of Angela's boys were wearing black trousers, white shirts, and black ties. As always, when Damian spotted me, he gave a sweet smile. I smiled back. Tevin hesitated when he came by. "I'm an usher!" he whispered with a pleased expression on his face. My heart skipped a beat. You're one of God's little miracles too! I thought.

LUKE 18:15–17 (TLB) *One day some mothers brought their babies to him to touch and bless. But the disciples told them to go away. Then Jesus called the children over to him and said to the disciples, "Let the little children come to me! Never send them away: For the Kingdom of God belongs to men who have hearts as trusting as these little children's. And anyone who doesn't have their kind of faith will never get within the Kingdom's gates."*

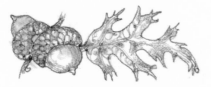

God's Little Mystery

ROMANS 8:15 (NKJV) *For you did not receive the spirit of bondage again to fear, but you received the Spirit of adoption by whom we cry out, "Abba, Father."*

One Sunday morning, after a freezing rain, our three teenage sons and I headed for church. It was our middle son Scott's turn to drive. "Be careful," he told us after warming up the engine. "It's slippery out here." Brian, our oldest, got in next to Scott. Myles and I sat in back. Then Scott turned the car out of our driveway.

Immediately the vehicle slid to the right across the top of our hill and into a gutter. "Stay inside, Mom," said Scott. Then he and his brothers tried to figure out how to get the automobile back on the road. All of them were having trouble staying on their feet.

"Myles," I said after a short while, "go get your dad." Lord, please help, I prayed when Jerry came sliding toward us. Then he looked about. "Here's your problem," my husband announced, tugging at a little log wedged under a front right wheel. After freeing it, Jerry tossed it aside onto an embankment.

All of a sudden, even though the emergency brake was on, the car started moving. "Oh, God!" I cried from the rear seat. Scott and Brian were in front with their arms outstretched across the hood. Neither our sons nor I can recall if they were attempting to stop the car or trying to hold on. I desperately reached for the steering wheel, but it was too far away. Although I feared the worst, I kept calling out to our Creator.

Suddenly the vehicle stopped. It had traveled one car length. Thank you, I prayed as Brian and Scott got on their feet. When Jerry and Myles reached us, my husband looked under the car. Again he found a little log, beneath the right back tire.

LAMENTATIONS 3:23 (TLB) *Great is his faithfulness; his loving kindness begins afresh each day.*

The Terracotta Fiat

PSALM 85:10 (KJV) *Mercy and truth are met together; righteousness and peace have kissed each other.*

"Mom, want to go for a ride?" said Brian with a wide grin. He and his dad had just purchased Brian's first car. By saving his summer wages, our seventeen-year-old was now the proud owner of a used 1976 Fiat, and he was eager for me to see how well his vehicle could perform.

"Certainly," I said. We were especially pleased because our three boys would no longer need to borrow our new Pontiac— Brian was willing to share his "wheels." Many years have gone by since our boys took the Pontiac without permission. Upon reminiscing with them about this incident, I confirmed several facts. Each one thought that one of the others had asked. They had planned to triple date. The Fiat was a four seater. They wanted to impress girls. They forgot to double-check with Mom or Dad.

"Let's switch cars on them," Jerry and I said, laughing, when we found out. "That will teach them a lesson." We knew they were at a church drama club rehearsal. "Won't they be surprised," we said, "when they step outside." Then I watched as Jerry got in Brian's car and drove away.

Moments afterward a nerve shattering bang filled the air. "Oh, God!" I cried. With trembling insides I ran down our steep driveway. At a blind curve I found Jerry and a neighbor surveying damages. The other car had suffered a tiny dent. However, Brian's Fiat was totaled. "Thank you, Lord," I said, after seeing that no one was hurt. All of the Pinkney family felt awful. Right away I began looking for a replacement car.

"A 1978 Fiat in good condition," I told Brian after a few weeks of searching PennySaver ads. So, with much hope, we went to see it. To our surprise we found a terracotta Fiat almost identical to the one lost. "Thank you, Lord!" I exclaimed.

PSALM 27:13 (NIV) *I am confident of this: I will see the goodness of the Lord in the land of the living.*

Shadow's Shadow

PSALM 30:5 B (NKJV) *His favor is for life; Weeping may endure for a night, But joy comes in the morning.*

Many good and also sad memories come to mind when I remember Shadow, our family cat for eleven years. He was a jet black feline with bright, alert yellow eyes. It was due to our first grandchild Gloria Nicole's love of Shadow, and his attachment to her, when she was living with us, that inspired me to try writing.

Losing him one Christmas Eve was a deeply painful experience. Over the last few years preceding his death, our pet profoundly missed the attention he had received when our grandchild lived with us. And what made matters worse, Jerry and I were often away on author visits.

How was I to tell his favorite friend, or the rest of the grandchildren? They were all expected home for Christmas. So we decided to wait until after the holiday.

A few days before the New Year, Gloria Nicole and I were in a local shopping center. "Mom-Mom," she said, staring at a pet store window, "I have seven dollars. Is that enough to buy a kitten?" I said a silent prayer. Then she added, "What happened to Shadow? Did he die?"

I knew that it was time to tell her. "Yes," I said softly. "Shadow was very sick." Well, she held back her grief until we got into my car.

Then big tears came rushing down. "But," cried Gloria Nicole, "will I ever see him again?"

What should I say now? I wondered. "You'll see him in heaven," I responded, wiping her tears.

Instantly Gloria Nicole stopped crying. "In heaven?" she said with a questioning look on her face. "By the time I get there, Shadow's hair will have turned all white, and I won't recognize him!"

"Don't worry," I told her, holding back a smile. "You'll see Shadow again." Then Gloria Nicole became quiet. She seemed to be satisfied with my answer.

In the Valentine season following the loss of Shadow, our daughter, Troy, and son-in-love (as I prefer to call him), Leon, decided to give Gloria Nicole a kitten. It was a difficult decision because the three of them suffer with allergies. They were stepping out on faith.

I thought it a wonderful idea, for Gloria Nicole had told me that she was praying for a kitten of her own. However, Valentine's Day is a popular time to give a cat. There didn't appear to be one left in the pet shops or at the local animal shelter.

Finally, after many telephone calls, a kitten was located in a New Rochelle shelter. "Hurry," the man said after Troy's desperate plea for Gloria Nicole. "I have many requests but have only one kitten. I'll try to hold it for you."

With hope in their hearts, daughter and granddaughter arrived at the shelter. After identifying themselves, they were ushered into a back room. There sat a tiny jet black kitten with alert yellow eyes who was born during the Christmas holidays. "What will you name her?" asked Troy as Gloria Nicole snuggled with her very own pet.

"Pumpkin!" she exclaimed.

ISAIAH 38:19 (TAB) *The living, the living—they shall thank and praise You, as I do this day; the father shall make known to the children Your faithfulness and Your truth.*

The Cape Cod Crickets

PSALM 150:6 (TLB) *Let everything alive give praises to the Lord! You praise him! Hallelujah!*

How wonderful it felt to be alone for one week in a rented house on Cape Cod. "Solitude is just what I need for writing," I had told Jerry before he and our family went home. However, that evening at dusk a lone cricket made its presence known. Later, during the night, it crept from room to room in concert. "How is a person supposed to sleep?" I called out.

Thanks to Jerry, I have almost overcome my dread of big bugs. He taught me how to capture harmless insects with a cup and cardboard, then free them outdoors. Yet this one kept eluding me. One night its sound was so shrill that I put on earphones, but its chirruping pierced my music.

Finally I went home. "Now for a good sleep," I exclaimed as I crawled into bed. Suddenly a lone cricket's serenade rang out from the room where I had unpacked. "Was there a cricket here before tonight?" I said. Jerry assured me there hadn't been. After calming myself, I recalled leaving a satchel open overnight before leaving the Cape.

Our visitor performed several days and nights, then abruptly stopped. One morning I found it at the top of a second floor landing on its back with legs stiffened by death. At an earlier time in my life I would have felt relieved. However, at that moment I changed. Crickets are one of God's creatures, I thought. Life is so precious!

"This house is a blessing," we exclaimed the following summer when settling into another rented home on Cape Cod. To our delight it was nestled in a grove of trees that had numerous species of birdlife. After a careful inspection, I discovered that the only cricket there seemed content under a washing machine in the basement.

Fortunately the creature stayed there. So after two relatively quiet weeks we returned home feeling rested. But as soon as lights were turned off, a lone cricket sounded from the living room. "This can't be!" I said. Jerry fell promptly asleep.

For what seemed like hours I lay awake listening to the cricket's song, then decided to pray. "Lord," I whispered, "that bug is somewhere near my devotional window. I want to get up early. Please make it go outdoors!"

"Thank you, Jesus," I said the next morning. For our friend had taken itself into the dining room. I was able to study the Scriptures in peace, but not in quiet. Later Jerry remembered a new sonic device, which we had purchased before going away, that forces creatures outside. Right away it exited through a hole that leads into an attached greenhouse. Then, among our plants, the Cape Cod cricket found a harmonious place to chirp.

A few months later, after presenting to a kindergarten class in Mount Vernon, New York, a child asked about my next book. Then I shared the telling of "The Cape Cod Crickets." I had a small paper box with me that day (discovered in a toy store soon after our vacation) with two tin crickets inside.

Now, up to that moment whenever the box was opened, the tin crickets would make a realistic chirruping sound. However, that day it was silent. Oh, my goodness! I thought as the children watched with expectant looks on their faces. Lord, I thought, what's wrong? So I tried chirruping, but gave a poor imitation. "Maybe if we pray, it will work," I said afterward. Right at that moment the tin crickets commenced to making their usual sound. All present, including me, were startled. "Who prayed?" I said.

Immediately a little boy sitting on the floor up front raised his hand with a big smile. "I did!" he said excitedly. Thanks, Lord, I silently prayed. You care about everything in the lives of your children.

LUKE 9:47o–48 (TAB) *But, Jesus, as He perceived the thoughts of their hearts, took a little child and put him at His side And told them, Whoever receives and accepts and welcomes this child in My name and for My sake receives and accepts and welcomes Me; and whoever so receives Me so also receives Him Who sent Me; for he who is least and lowliest among you all—he is (the one who is truly) great.*

Something Real

ROMANS 8:24–25 (NRSV) *For in hope we were saved. Now hope that is seen is not hope. For who hopes for what is seen? But if we hope for what we do not see, we wait for it with patience.*

"Will you be my prayer partner?" an usher at The Star of Bethlehem Missionary Baptist Church asked one Sunday after service. It was the fall of 1995. Her name was Ellen Geraldine Ballard. I knew her as Gerri. Up to that moment I had no knowledge of prayer partnerships. However, I had a gut feeling that it would require work. Looking into her bright eyes and wide grin, I thought, Lord, I already have so much that you have given me to do.

"Certainly, Gerri," I replied. "But what is a prayer partner?"

"Oh, someone to call you every now and then," she responded with an even bigger smile. "Sometimes we'll pray. Some days just talk." That was the first day of a miraculous journey with our Lord Jesus Christ.

Only our Creator knew then that Gerri, who was a dialysis patient, would soon become critically ill—so sick that she would require nursing home care. It was a joy to visit her weekly with prayers, the Holy Scriptures, and inspirational songs.

I will never forget the day that the doctors told Gerri's father, Deacon Horton (who was constantly by her side), and Pastor Arthur Lewter that she was slipping away. However, deep within my heart I believed that our Lord would heal Gerri.

Many, many prayers went up from The Star of Bethlehem Missionary Baptist Church and Gerri's numerous other friends. Soon God answered with a miracle. After the amputation of an infected leg, Gerri was herself again, filled with Jesus' joy.

"Gerri," I told her when she was recuperating, "your life brings to mind an old tune from the seventies." Then I sang "Gimme Something Real" for her.

"Glory Jean," she responded (addressing me by the name that she saved for special moments), "I really like that song a lot. I can relate," Gerri said, laughing. "Maybe you can find me a tape."

"I'll try," was my response. It's pretty old, I thought, leaving the nursing home, I'll never find it. Then I headed for a local record store.

"Herbie," I said, greeting the owner, "do you have 'Gimme Something Real' by Ashford and Simpson?" He looked at me with raised eyebrows.

"Mrs. Pinkney," said Herbie, "that album came out a long time ago. But I'll look in my catalog. Maybe it's been released on CD." I watched with hope as he checked and rechecked. "Sorry," he finally said, "it's not listed."

"Well," I responded, "I'll just browse." As I turned around, my eyes immediately fell upon an old corrugated box. Inside it were vertically stacked cassette tapes. Without hesitation, I reached in and pulled out a single tape with two familiar faces on its casing. It was Nick Ashford and Valerie Simpson..."Gimme Something Real." "Where did these tapes come from?" I said excitedly.

Herbie stared at the tape I was holding in disbelief. "A friend was cleaning house," he explained. "I just put that box there in case someone might want one."

"The Lord led you to do this for Gerri Ballard," I answered, feeling in awe of our God from my head to my toes.

Thanks be to our gracious Lord Jesus Christ, my prayer partner Gerri, after being granted a miracle healing, left the nursing home, lived for an extended time, then fell asleep in Christ.

PSALM 118:23 (NLT) *This is the Lord's doing, and it is marvelous to see.*

On Bended Knees

PHILIPPIANS 2:9–11 (KJV) *Wherefore God also hath highly exalted him, and given him a name which is above every name: That at the name of Jesus every knee should bow, of things in heaven, and things in earth, and things under the earth; And that every tongue should confess that Jesus Christ is Lord, to the glory of God the Father.*

One morning after devotionals, a crystal clear message came: There are times when we must kneel in prayer. Later that day I was asked to drive my friend and prayer partner Minister Linda C. to the hospital where she was to have minor surgery. On the way I told her what I had heard from our Lord about praying.

"But I can't pray on my knees," she explained. Because of illness, her body is very delicate, making it necessary for Minister Linda to walk with a cane. Movement for her is extremely laborious, yet I wondered if praying in a kneeling position (because of the sacrifice) might bring more blessings from our Lord. Then, just a short time later, I had an eye-opening experience and an answer.

When we arrived at the hospital, a nurse who introduced herself as Nurse Linda promptly began hooking Minister Linda up to an IV. As soon as I heard her name, I knew it was one of God's twin signposts to let us know that he was with us. Then trouble came. My friend has tiny veins, and so her nurse was unable to insert a needle even after several attempts.

I was seated at the foot of Minister Linda's bed, holding on to my *Spirit-Filled Life Bible* while silently praying. Please, Lord, I pleaded, make that needle go in! All of a sudden my eyes focused on a metal plate that was mounted on the footboard. The word knee was there. "Yes, Lord," I whispered, then went into the washroom, got on my knees, and prayed.

"It just slipped right in!" said Nurse Linda with a relieved look on her face when I came back. Oh, thank you, Lord Jesus, I prayed silently. Afterward I told them about the metal plate that had been revealed. "It reminded me about intercessory prayers," I said.

Later, while writing this accounting, a second thought came on the subject of intercessory praying. It is one that I hope to remember always: Those who are able should never forget to bow down for those who cannot.

ROMANS 12:6–7 (NLT) *God has given each of us the ability to do certain things well. So if God has given you the ability to prophesy, speak out when you have faith that God is speaking through you. If your gift is that of serving others, serve them well.*

Alan and Jerry's Gifts

MATTHEW 10:27 (TAB) *What I say to you in the dark, tell, in the light; and what you hear whispered in the ear, proclaim upon the housetops.*

Take a back road to the church house, came as an overwhelming thought. This happened one Saturday morning after I had purchased a copy of *Small Miracles* at a local bookstore. Off I went to my third home church, The Star of Bethlehem Missionary Baptist. The lot was empty.

Just as I was parking, another car came through its gates. "Hey, Glo," called Gloria M. as she got out. "What are you doing here?"

"I'm not sure," I responded, feeling baffled by the locked doors. "I feel as if the Lord told me to come."

My friend raised an eyebrow. "Well," she said, showing me her key, "I'm going inside to cook."

Suddenly an idea surfaced. "I'll go to the sanctuary and pray," I announced, following Gloria M. Then I went upstairs and knelt before the altar. Lord, I began, I don't know why you have sent me to Star today, but here I am. Please tell me what you would have me to do. Amen.

Then after saying good-bye to my friend, I headed homeward. There is a supermarket close to our house. Just as I approached it, our Lord gave a second message: Go buy Jerry a duck. That's a good idea, I thought. Roast duckling is one of his favorites. So I went in.

Afterward a third message came: Take Jerry flowers. So I headed to a florist and selected a mixed bouquet. White flowers only, came the fourth message. Promptly I changed to an assortment of white blooms. Most of them were opened. However, a few buds were not.

Finally I drove home. We live in an older house that has an antiquated garage door. As usual, I beeped the car horn for Jerry to open it. The instant I saw his face, my heart began to race. "Alan died this morning," he said softly. With flowers and duckling in hand, Jerry and I hugged each other. We had just lost a good friend, and Jerry's closest contemporary in the field of illustration.

That next morning while I was at church, Jerry sat in the parlor recalling our long friendship with the Cober family, and thinking of Alan's contributions as an artist. "The sun came through a window, and the flower buds opened," Jerry told me when I came back. He had a peaceful look on his face. Thank you, Lord, I thought.

Then, on the afternoon of Alan's service, another miraculous thing happened. We were standing before our kitchen window remarking on the lovely memorial service that Alan's wife, Ellen, had prepared. All of a sudden a flock of sand-colored doves landed directly beneath us. Jerry and I were astonished. They gathered on the ground for a moment, then in three risings flew away. Yet a few stayed for a while.

Several days later Jerry and I were at a dinner party where we talked about our extraordinary visitation. "Never had we seen so many morning doves," I said.

Our hostess, Renata R., looked puzzled. "Are you saying *morning* or *mourning* doves?" she asked. Both of us gave the incorrect answer.

"They're not *morning* doves," our friend told us. "They're *mourning* doves, because of their mournful cooing sounds." Sent by our God to comfort, I thought.

DEUTERONOMY 33:26 (TAN) *O Jeshurun, there is none like God, Riding through the heavens to help you, Through the skies in His majesty.*

THE CREATOR

In the Name of God, the Compassionate, the Merciful
PRAISE BE TO GOD,
Creator of the heavens and the earth!
He sends forth the angels as His messengers,
with two, three or four pairs of wings.
He multiplies His creatures according to His will.
God has power over all things.
The blessings God bestows on men none can withold;
and what He withholds none can bestow, apart from Him.
He is the Mighty, the Wise One.

35:1–2
THE KORAN

Day of Graces

JOHN 14:23 (KJV) *Jesus answered and said unto him, If a man love me, he will keep my words: and my Father will love him, and we will come unto him, and make our abode with him.*

"I don't feel no ways tired. Come too far from where I started from. Nobody told me that the road would be easy. I don't believe He brought me this far to leave me." With these uplifting lyrics from a favored song, I shall attempt to humbly describe one Holy Spirit–filled day.

"Don't get upset," said my husband, Jerry, as he came into the kitchen with deep creases in his forehead, "I have something to tell you." I was about to prepare lunch, but stopped. He told me that a picture book had just been published using Ecclesiastes 3, which was the identical text that our son Myles and I had worked with more than a year earlier. Yet we were unsuccessful at obtaining a contract.

An awful chill came over me as I stared in disbelief. "How could this happen?" I said. Why, Lord? I wondered. Did we give up too quickly?

Jerry looked concerned. "Let's go out for lunch today," he suggested. "Maybe I can cheer you up." With a heavy heart I agreed. Suddenly a personal thought that I have expressed often came to mind: Ideas are in the air. They have wings. Use them or they will fly away. Then, with a deep feeling of gloom, I headed for Jerry's car.

Now, in one of my most treasured books, the first *Small Miracles*, Dr. Bernie Siegel writes of discovering pennies in peculiar places at needful times. I also find small coins or rubber bands. For me there is no doubt that these signposts are given by the Holy Spirit, the Comforter, to strengthen our trust in Jesus.

Therefore I was startled but not surprised when a gift lay on the passenger side of Jerry's car. "Where did this come from?" I exclaimed. There was the longest and widest rubber band that I had ever found. My face broke out in a grin.

"From The Art Shelf," said Jerry. After three decades of service, Gloria and Jim Scalzo, proprietors of our local art supply store, were closing. Jim had offered Jerry a handful of large rubber bands. "I didn't have a need for them," Jerry explained, "so I only took one and tossed it on the seat."

"Thanks," I responded, then put it on my wrist. "It's for me. Thank you, Lord," I whispered, then exclaimed, "God sure has a sense of humor!"

After lunch and much laughter about my newly found rubber band, I went to pick up Gloria Nicole and her friend Alexis from school. "I have a few stops to make," I told them. "Then we're going to the Barnes and Noble bookstore."

Well, the once dreaded picture book that is henceforth named Mystery Book was not on their shelves at the bookstore. "Sorry," said a salesperson. "We're all out." Ask her to look in back, came an unmistakable still, small voice. So I asked. "Perhaps there is one," the salesperson responded, then went to search. While she was gone, the girls and I browsed.

It wasn't long before I noticed something peculiar. "Gloria

and Alexis," I called, "there are no Pinkney books in the entire picture book section." Right then my salesperson came back with Mystery Book in hand. I thanked her, introduced myself, then told her about my discovery.

"I'll get someone to help you," the young lady said excitedly. She hurried away.

Within minutes a woman came toward us smiling over the rim of her glasses. Her name was Jane Hubrec. At that time she was the Community Relations Coordinator there. In Ms. Hubrec's hand was a stack of Pinkney books. "You've brought them out to show us," I said happily.

"Why, no," she replied with a surprised tone in her voice. "I've been on the telephone trying to find out how to get in touch with you. Your telephone number is unlisted." I stared in awe of God, only able to nod my head. "We want you here for a book signing," she explained. In complete joy I recovered quickly. "What made you come in today?" she asked.

"The Holy Spirit," I promptly answered with a brand-new boldness. Her eyes opened wide.

"Well," she said, sounding pleased, "if you had not stopped in, I would have had to find someone else. Our newsletter information is due by this evening." I was speechless. "Are you available October twenty-ninth for our Writers Harvest?" I agreed to call her later. I needed to check my calendar.

Lord, I silently prayed as I drove home, after all that has happened today, I'm sure this date must be free. Thank you for your blessings. Needless to say, our Lord God granted a blessed signing, a poster to remind Jerry and me of that event, and a flyer to show at author visits.

Now, dear readers, it is of the utmost importance for you to understand the significance of my jumbo rubber band: As my uncle Thomas Thompson of Goldsboro, North Carolina, might say, "Why, that elastic holds a stack of books right well!"

JOHN 4:34–35 (NIV) *"My food," said Jesus, "is to do the will of him who sent me and to finish his work. Do you not say, 'Four months more and then the harvest'? I tell you, open your eyes and look at the fields! They are ripe for harvest."*

First Day of Obadiah

MATTHEW 25:13 (NKJV) *"Watch therefore, for you know neither the day nor the hour in which the Son of Man is coming."*

"I asked the Lord to give us a speaker for our African-American Sunday Celebration," said Reverend Youlander Thompson. "He gave me your name."

"I'd love to come," was my spontaneous reply. Reverend Thompson, who is my cousin, was inviting me to First Orrum Missionary Baptist Church in Orrum, North Carolina, where she is pastor. Whenever possible I spend time with family in my birth state. "Would you like me to talk about my books?" I asked.

"Sister," she said, "we want you to speak on whatever the Lord places upon your heart."

I couldn't help smiling. "I'm going to ask him," I responded. So before going to bed, I made a prayer request. However, his answer didn't come that night. But early the next day I knelt in prayer as the sun was coming up. Afterward, with shut eyes, I held my *Spirit-Filled Life Bible* and asked, "Lord, please lead me to what you would have me to do." Then I opened to Obadiah. Now, this is not a simple thing to achieve, for in the Old Testament books, Obadiah is the shortest, having one chapter.

After studying it and the accompanying Bible guides, I felt perplexed. Obadiah, a minor prophet, is instructed by God in a vision to deliver a message. Verse 15 reads: "For the day of the Lord upon all the nations is near; As you have done, it shall be done to you; Your reprisal shall return upon your own head."

Lord, I'm not a preacher, I protested. Will the congregation accept such a strong message from me, an inexperienced layperson, about the day of judgment? Am I misunderstanding you? Please tell me again. What would you have me to do?"

An entire day went by without an answer. Howbeit, early the next morning, after meditation and prayer, I asked him a second time. With eyes closed and my hands upon an older Bible that our daughter, Troy, had given me, I opened to Obadiah.

Lord Jesus, I prayed, you told me that I am your prayer warrior, foot soldier, and goodly news teller, but this is too hard for me. Suddenly I remembered Gideon in the book of Judges. Gideon asked God for more than one sign of His Holy Will. Like me he needed extra assurance. Please make it clearer so I will understand, I added. Then I went about my daily chores.

Later that afternoon, while passing by our front parlor, I spotted a tiny, half-mooned piece of paper on the carpet in front of my prayer window. Pick it up, came a crystal clear thought, it's for you. Slowly I turned it over. "Yes, Lord!" I exclaimed. "Obadiah it is!" In my hand was an identification tab from the book of Obadiah. It had fallen from my aged Bible. Immediately I commenced to studying for a first sermonette, entitled "Mold a New Lifestyle."

That message is best described in the outline I made using my *Spirit-Filled Life Bible*. It describes "Day of the Lord" as a term used by the Old Testament prophets to signify a time in the history of mankind when God directly intervenes to bring salvation to his people and punishment to the rebellious. By it God restores his righteous order in the Earth.

I wrote about the need for people of God to care for

humankind as did Christ Jesus; and to live in a state of readiness for a visitation from our Lord. In a summation it said, "time is running out." Then with much fear of being disobedient, I began revising. Lord, I prayed, please help me write according to your will!

PSALM 19:7–9 (KJV) *The law of the LORD is perfect, converting the soul: the testimony of the LORD is sure, making wise the simple. The statutes of the LORD are right, rejoicing the heart: the commandment of the LORD is pure, enlightening the eyes. The fear of the LORD is clean, enduring for ever: the judgments of the LORD are true and righteous altogether.*

Second Day of Obadiah

PSALM 119:10–12 (NLT) *I have tried my best to find you—don't let me wander from your commands. I have hidden your word in my heart, that I might not sin against you. Blessed are you, O Lord; teach me your principles.*

"We're coming with you, Mom," said Troy Bernardette. To my delight she and our granddaughter Gloria Nicole had decided to accompany me to Orrum, North Carolina. "We don't want to miss your first sermonette, and we don't want you to go alone."

Then another blessing came. "Orrum and Myrtle Beach, South Carolina, are a short drive from each other," Reverend Thompson told me. "I'll make reservations," she said. With great anticipation I accepted her suggestion. Instantly a picture flooded my mind of my girls having a mini-vacation while I studied by the ocean.

Things were progressing smoothly with one exception: I couldn't settle on appropriate dress for a pulpit. Finally, on the night before leaving I prayed for divine guidance. It was the second time that I asked. Wear your ivory suit, came a crystal clear message. Days before, this very same answer had been revealed by the Holy Spirit. However, I became sidetracked after finding out that some of the congregation would be wearing African attire. "Thank you, Lord," I finally said.

Also, earlier that day during morning devotionals I had been led with shut eyes to I Corinthians 11:5 (NKJV). It is written, "But every woman who prays or prophesies with her head uncovered dishonors her head, for that is one and the same as if her head were shaved." Thank you, Lord, I prayed, I know it is your will for me to cover my head. I'll wear a turban.

Later that day I went to a local shopping center for fabric and two other items that were needed for my trip. Holy Spirit of the living God, I prayed before entering Steinbach department store, please lead me to what I'm looking for. The store was having a Going Out of Business sale. "All I need is a full-length ivory slip and a pair of black slippers in size eight. Don't let me become distracted!" Within moments I found both items. However, the slippers were size ten. Get them anyway, came an overwhelming message. Oh well, I thought, thick socks will make them fit snugly and keep my feet warm.

Promptly I headed for a checkout counter, but a clearance rack filled with bargains got my attention. It won't hurt to browse a little, I decided. Suddenly the department store's piped-in music system became louder. One song ended and another began. My mouth fell open as an old rock song entitled "Gloria" played. I couldn't help laughing. God surely has a sense of humor, I thought. Then I hurriedly paid a cashier, and headed for the door as my name was spelled out letter by letter.

Thank you, Holy Spirit, I prayed. I asked you to keep me from distractions, and you have!

Lastly I headed for JoAnn Fabrics and Crafts. Lord, I prayed while getting out of my car, sometimes stretch knits are hard to find. Please help. Instantly I spotted an oversized gum-ball machine with super-sized yellow gum balls in the shop's entryway. Thank you, Lord, for a yellow color of hope signpost! I prayed. Then, within minutes, I found an aisle with an array of colored stretch cloths including ivory. Now, I thought after making my purchase, according to your will, O Lord, my head will be covered when I step onto your pulpit.

2 CHRONICLES 7:14 (KJV) *If my people, which are called by my name, shall humble themselves, and pray, and seek my face, and turn from their wicked ways; then will I hear from heaven, and will forgive their sin, and will heal their land.*

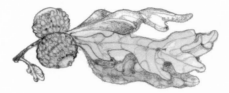

Third Day of Obadiah

AMOS 5:21–24 (TEV) *The Lord says, "I hate your religious festivals; I cannot stand them! When you bring me burnt offerings and grain offerings, I will not accept them; I will not accept the animals you have fattened to bring me as offerings. Stop your noisy songs; I do not want to listen to your harps. Instead, let justice flow like a stream, and righteousness like a river that never goes dry."*

One morning while working on this manuscript I opened a medicine cabinet to get my toothbrush. Suddenly a box of throat lozenges fell from the top shelf, hit a wall, then landed on the floor. Holy Spirit, are you telling me that I'm going to have a sore throat? I wondered. So, I tucked them in a pocket. Right then a crystal clear thought surfaced: You haven't written "Third Day of Obadiah." "Thank you, Lord!" I said.

It happened almost the same way on that night before leaving for Orrum, North Carolina, by way of Myrtle Beach, South Carolina. After returning home from shopping, I opened a medicine cabinet to get essentials for my trip. Instantly a box of Benadryl fell from a top shelf, hit the sink, then landed at my feet. You're telling me to pack Benadryl, aren't you, Lord? I thought, then packed it along with my *Spirit-Filled Life Bible*, new ivory slip, ivory fabric, and size ten slippers.

The next day our daughter, Troy Bernardette, her daughter, Gloria Nicole, and I checked into an oceanside motel in Myrtle

Beach. Our Lord blessed us with pleasant rooms, sunny skies, and warm temperatures. Right away the girls began exploring, while I spent my days staring at the sea, praying, studying, and rewriting that first sermonette.

Then on Friday evening something miraculous took place. "You two go and eat without me," I told them. Sunday was fast approaching, and I was still trying to perfect the Obadiah sermonette. Not long after the girls left, there was a knock at the door.

"Mom," said Troy Bernardette when she and her daughter came in, "Gloria has stomach cramps. I'm wondering if there may have been a fish stock in her pasta."

Gloria Nicole is highly allergic to bonefish, yet has always been able to eat shellfish. After the three of us prayed for a healing, they went to their room. Shortly afterward the telephone rang. "Mom, Gloria is breaking out in hives. She looks as if she might have an asthma attack."

"Do you have Benadryl?" I asked.

Troy sighed. "I have a bag full of medicines," she said, "but not that one."

"I've got Benadryl!" I said. We waited a short while after giving Gloria the antihistamine, but the thirteen-year-old wasn't getting better. Suddenly Troy and I knew that a hospital was needed. However, there was a graveled yard between our rooms and the rental car. It presented a new problem because Gloria's feet were so swollen that her shoes no longer fit. "I have size ten slippers in my room!" I announced.

Much praying went on as we got lost, then found a hospital. Thank you, Lord, I prayed as mother and daughter rushed into an emergency ward. "Where are they?" I asked after parking.

"You got her here just in time," said a nurse with a grave expression on her face. Then she led me to a back room. There lay Gloria Nicole hooked up to an IV containing more Benadryl, and wearing an oxygen mask. Immediately Troy and I thanked God for his mercy and grace.

Things were normal again on Saturday. Gloria Nicole was a little tired, but she was feeling fine. So I continued revising the sermonette. Then very early Sunday morning a message came: Throw it all away, said his still, small voice. I'll show you what to say. Therefore, I was led to use Post-its for marking other verses relating to the "Day of the Lord" prophesy found in the book of Obadiah.

"If a robin can say thank you, you can do it too!" sang the gospel choir at First Orrum Missionary Baptist Church. Immediately the sanctuary was filled with the presence of the Holy Spirit. Lord, I thought as I sat in the pastor's chair remembering the Hinds' Feet Scripture. This is a high place. Thank you for bringing your servant Gloria here.

Then the service was opened for personal testimonies. Troy Bernardette was one of the first to stand up. Everyone listened in awe of God while my daughter spoke about Gloria Nicole's allergy and asthma attack. "Praise the Lord!" Troy exclaimed.

Reverend Youlander Thompson gave an introduction. "One thing that I can say about my cousin," she concluded in her warm southern way of orating, "she's obedient."

After opening with a prayer, I spoke about the Day of our Lord Jesus Christ's return. In addition to Obadiah, the Lord had directed me to other days of divine retribution and restitution Scriptures. In summation I asked, "Will our homes be in order when Jesus comes? Or, will we have to say, 'Wait, Lord, until I change the channel on my TV' or 'Wait, Lord, until I change the music that I've been listening to' or 'Wait, Lord, until I get rid of the ungodly things in my life'?"

Then I showed them a memory box from my collection (containing mementos related to Godly incidents) and shared true tellings from this book. Finally, I closed with the last prophecy given by our God's servant Obadiah. It is recorded at the end of this accounting. Thank you, Father, I prayed silently as I sat down amid the First Orrum Missionary Baptist Church's resounding Amens!

OBADIAH 1:21 (NKJV) *Then saviors shall come to Mount Zion to judge the mountains of Esau, And the kingdom shall be the LORD's.*

God of Second Chance

PSALM 46:10 (NIV) *"Be still, and know that I am God; I will be exalted among the nations, I will be exalted in the earth."*

Reverend Arthur Lewter, the pastor of The Star of Bethlehem Missionary Baptist Church, has a saying that fittingly describes the following telling. "What a time, what a time!" he exclaims when speaking about journeying with our Lord. Here is what happened one morning while driving through Briarcliff Manor, New York.

Our Lord the Holy Spirit spoke these words: Visit this church. Jerry is going to like it! Immediately I told Gloria Nicole. We had been admiring the stained-glass windows of Briarcliff Congregational Church while en route to a summer arts camp at Pace University.

How curious it is that I had asked our Lord two years prior, by writing in a prayer journal, for a day when Jerry and I would worship side by side. Also, many believers had been praying for us. It was a deep concern, yet I was reluctant to obey the Spirit's revelation. (But, Lord, I protested, I don't have time now to visit that church. I'm away from Star too much. After all, I'm an officer and in the choir.) So I kept putting it off. Then Gloria Nicole's summer camp ended and our family headed for Cape Cod.

It was the weekend of Hurricane Bonnie. "The storm's coming!" a stranger announced when we stopped at a Lower Cape store. "Been living here all my life," the white-haired gentleman said, looking up at the clouds. I commenced to praying. We couldn't help remembering previous hurricanes while vacationing on the peninsula that is known as the "long arm of the sea." Please, Lord, I prayed, not another one!

On Sunday I was determined to visit a church despite the predicted hurricane. While searching through a telephone book, I found a signpost: Reverend Bonnie Goodwin, Christian Union Church. "I'll go there," I said. How startling it was to find myself in the same sanctuary that I had visited a year earlier.

"I know you have all come to hear Reverend Bonnie," said a deacon, "but she's away." Instantly a feeling of spiritual enlightenment washed over me. That storm is away too, I thought. Isn't it, Lord? "This morning," the deacon announced, "our guest minister is Reverend George Higgins."

I listened in disbelief as Reverend Higgins talked about places near our home in Westchester County, New York. Then the minister mentioned his previous church, The Briarcliff Congregational in Briarcliff Manor. Oh, Lord! I silently repented. Please forgive me. Thank you for a second chance. I'm going to visit that church as soon as I get home!

"I want to speak with you," Reverend Higgins said after service when I introduced myself. "An old African American preacher," he later told me, "used to minister to inmates at the correctional facility in Ossining, New York."

"Are you speaking of Reverend Louis Jernigan?" I said excitedly. The minister's face lit up. "Is he alive?" asked Reverend Higgins. Then I told him about the birthday card that I had mailed a day earlier in celebration of the elder minister's ninety-first year. Reverend Louis Jernigan is assistant to the pastor at The Star of

Bethlehem Missionary Baptist Church, where I had been a member for twenty-five years. In my mind it is no coincidence that the post office is located across the street from Christian Union Church.

Well, as Minister Nellie Johnson of Star always says, "Look at God!" By his merciful grace, Hurricane Bonnie passed over Cape Cod, and I visited The Briarcliff Congregational Church, a member of The United Church of Christ, as soon as I returned home.

To my delight, Jerry soon agreed to go with me. After that I began attending Star's Sunday school for forty-five minutes, then I'd leave to meet Jerry for the 10:00 to 11:00 A.M. service at Briarcliff. Afterward, since Star Church was not far away, I could reach that worship service by 11:15. Jerry and I were regularly attending services at Briarcliff. Everything had fallen neatly into place. At least, that's what I thought!

PROVERBS 16:9 (TAB) *A man's mind plans his way, but the Lord directs his steps and makes them sure.*

The First Bishop

MARK 1:1–2 (NKJV) *The beginning of the gospel of Jesus Christ, the Son of God. As it is written in the Prophets: "Behold, I send My messenger before Your face, Who will prepare Your way before You."*

Jerry and I were on our way to The Art Institute of Chicago, where he was to have a one-man show of his drawings and paintings for *Back Home* and *The Talking Eggs*. Uh-oh! I thought as we headed toward our seats. This person must be afraid of flying. For the snowy-haired man who was sitting in the aisle seat on our row had leaned back just long enough for me and Jerry to slip by. Then the elderly gentleman sat up until the plane was airborne. Right afterward he resumed his original position, that of holding his forehead in his hand.

Later a stewardess offered refreshments. Jerry and I ordered cocktails. However, the man said, "No, thank you," then went back to holding his head down. We're in for a rough trip, I thought. At long last he straightened up. Then he gave us a radiant smile. "I'm Bishop James H. Mayo," he announced, extending a warm bear-sized hand. "I'm on a pilgrimage with my flock. They're sitting farther back," he explained. Then Jerry introduced the two of us. "What brings you to Chicago?" asked the bishop.

I felt grateful that Jerry was answering Bishop Mayo's questions because I was feeling deeply ashamed. Also, I suspected that we were reeking of liquor. Forgive me, Lord, I prayed silently, for misjudging your servant. He was praying. And please forgive me for having an alcoholic beverage when you have shown me over and over again, through my daily Scriptures, that it is not your will for Gloria Jean. Suddenly the bishop turned toward me. "Do you have any of your books with you?" he asked.

Gratefully I handed him a copy of *Back Home*. At least I won't have to talk for a while, I thought. Then Bishop Mayo leaned on an elbow, carefully reading and studying each page. At long last he finished, with much praise for Jerry's illustrations.

Finally, his twinkling eyes focused on me. "Sister," he said, "you should be writing for the Lord!" I'm not planning to write for the Lord, I thought. Then after jotting down the name of a friend who was a Sunday school publisher in Tennessee, he gave me his card. "When you're ready," added the bishop, "give him my name." Neither Jerry nor I realized it then, but we were in the company of a prophet from God who knew that I was being called to change my unacceptable ways, and commit my works to our Lord.

ACTS 2:39 (NRSV) *For the promise is for you, for your children, and for all who are far away, everyone whom the Lord our God calls to him.*

The Second Bishop

I SAMUEL 12:23–24 (NKJV) *Moreover, as for me, far be it from me that I should sin against the LORD in ceasing to pray for you; but I will teach you the good and the right way. Only fear the LORD, and serve Him in truth with all your heart; for consider what great things He has done for you.*

I met Bishop Roderick R. Caesar and his wife, Beverly Caesar, the pastor and associate pastor of Bethel Gospel Tabernacle of Jamaica Queens, New York, when the three of us appeared on Trinity Broadcasting's *Praise the Lord* show. It was the winter of 1997. In the interview, I described my way of creating stories as "rewriting history." My goal at that time was to create fictional tales for children, centered around the violent death of my mother when I was eight. I didn't realize that my writing had become a struggle between truth and fiction.

Near the end of that show Pastor Beverly prayed for the viewing audience. Then Bishop Roderick Caesar said:

> "Lord, we pray for Gloria as she writes under the inspiration
> of the Holy Spirit.
> That you would give wisdom and grace....
> That she would do what you would have her do.
> Give her boldness to stand upon your truth and believe
> you for the results....

And I pray that her works will fall into the hands of people who are needy for the truth....
And, that it will be the beginning of a pilgrimage of many to receive you into their life as Lord and Savior....
For what you are going to do through her ministries ...
And through the medium of her work, we thank you ...
And we praise you. Amen."

It took more than a year before I knew that our Lord Jesus Christ was, through the bishop's prayer, calling me to write only for him.

I PETER 1:15–16 (KJV) *But as he which hath called you is holy, so be ye holy in all manner of conversation; Because it is written, Be ye holy; for I am holy.*

The Third Bishop

MARK 11:9 (NKJV) *Then those who went before and those who followed cried out, saying: "'Hosanna! Blessed is He who comes in the name of the Lord!'"*

How blessed it was for my prayer partner Rose and me to worship with Evangelist Benny Hinn. It was estimated that eighteen thousand people were present that morning at the Meadowlands sports complex in New Jersey. My first knowledge of this anointed man happened early one morning when I was led by the Holy Spirit to turn on the television set. Soon afterward a purple binding in a bookstore sale bin, entitled *The Anointing*, got my attention. In it Benny Hinn's personal relationship with the Holy Spirit is so riveting that I could only digest one chapter at a time.

How right it was for a gentleman who told us that he was a minister to sit between me and Rose. Zeal for our Lord prompted the three of us to begin talking long before formal introductions. We were instantly caught up in sharing personal testimonies of our God. Right away I told him how the Lord had led me to find the right church for my husband, Jerry. Afterward our new friend fell silent. At long last he turned toward me.

"Sister," he began, "the Lord has told me to tell you something." Instantly feelings of dread surfaced. "Our God is a God of oneness," said the minister. "He doesn't want you worshiping in one church and your husband worshiping in another."

For the first time I accepted the Lord's will, as tears welled inside of me. "He's been telling me that for some time now," I responded. "But it's been twenty-five years at my church. And I'm an officer. How can I leave? Yes," I said, "I've been resisting."

The minister looked compassionate. "I suspect," he responded, "either your husband will join your church, or you'll join his."

How reassuring it is to know how much God loves his children, so much that he graces us with more than one chance to obey. Near the end of that miracle crusade, Benny Hinn invited all ministers to come forward. Our new friend got up to go. "Do you have a card?" I asked. "Maybe we can become prayer partners." Then he handed us yellow cards.

For a second neither Rose nor I could believe it. "Bishop John H. Mayo," it said. Quickly I told him about the elder bishop's prophesy. "I'm almost certain that his name was also Mayo." He looked curious. "I had not begun writing for our Lord then," I admitted, "but I am now. I've committed my works to him." Rose and the bishop smiled. Then he shook our hands and hurried toward the stage. Unfortunately, we had to leave before he returned.

"I feel the Holy Spirit's presence in here," Rose exclaimed, pointing to her heart as we headed for my car. "Do you?" she asked. I smiled from my head to the soles of my feet. Both of us had come away with more than we had hoped for.

Once I was back home, the elder minister's card was another confirmation. Promptly I telephoned Rose, then the younger bishop. At first it was puzzling to learn that there were no family ties between the two Mayos. Nonetheless, they and Bishop Caesar are three brothers in Christ. And all were sent by him with a prophesy.

Hours passed before another realization came. "What a silly dream," I had told Jerry at breakfast on the morning of Benny

Hinn's miracle crusade. "It was so real. It seems as if I spent most of my night searching for a bottle of mayo!"

MARK 16:20 (NRSV) *And they went out and proclaimed the good news everywhere, while the Lord worked with them and confirmed the message by the signs that accompanied it.*

Mourning Has Broken

PSALM 42:8 (NRSV) *By day the LORD commands his steadfast love, and at night his song is with me, a prayer to the God of my life.*

One dawning our Lord awoke me with a melody. For a while I lay in bed silently singing "Morning Has Broken." We have that song on an album by Cat Stevens, I thought, wondering if it were still in our attic. However, after a thorough search I was unable to locate it. Then for many days its gentle lyrics continued to surface at sunrise. "Jerry, there must be a reason why this is happening," I said. He suggested that I look for the tune on a compact disc. Finally, after I purchased *Cat Stevens' Greatest Hits* with "Morning Has Broken" as its eleventh song, the melody at dawn ceased.

Then one Sunday something unusual occurred. "I can't go to Briarcliff Church with you today, Jerry," I said. I was still a member at The Star of Bethlehem, and had been running back and forth between two services. "There's a lot taking place at Star today," I told him. Right then the Holy Spirit spoke: You asked for a time when the two of you would worship side by side. You asked. . . . I answered. . . . You go!

We arrived just before the choir entered the back of Briarcliff's sanctuary, followed by Reverend David Powers. Then, as always, they began singing. Jerry and I sat, expecting to hear a customary prelude such as "Canon from Partita on St. Anne."

Instead they sang the Gaelic hymn "Morning Has Broken." I could barely maintain the stillness that is a nurturing part of their worship service. "Jerry," I said softly, then nudged him. "Do you hear?" He nodded. "Look," I said later, after searching and finding the hymn in Briarcliff's songbook. "Our God is awesome!" I whispered.

That following Sunday it was another full day for me at Star. Again I heard the same message: You asked.... I answered.... You go! Then as Jerry and I waited in stillness for the worship service at Briarcliff to begin, the choir sang its opening prelude. "This can't be happening," I whispered as "Morning Has Broken" filled their sanctuary. "They have never sung the same song two Sundays in a row before," I said. Jerry nodded with a deepening crease in his forehead.

"That can't be," Reverend David Powers said when we told him after church. "They never sing the same selection twice in succession." Jerry and I looked at each other. Then in bewilderment I headed for Star.

Not long afterward Reverend Powers solved the divine mystery. "The choir did sing 'Morning Has Broken' two Sundays in a row," he explained. At first he had thought it to be a mistake. But later he learned that there had not been a choir rehearsal that week. "Therefore," he said, "they sang the song from the previous Sunday." Lord, I wondered, pondering these incredible events, what does it all mean?

Then, late one morning not long afterward, I went to Creative Copy, our local copy shop, to pick up a telling for my manuscript. Upon leaving I noticed that a new bookstore had opened. Go in, came a crystal clear thought. Immediately a lovely illustration of the Virgin Mary on a book jacket got my attention. For some time prior to this our Lord Jesus had placed it upon my heart to honor his mother, Mary. Promptly I purchased *Gifts of Grace*, a gathering of personal encounters with the Virgin Mary by Lone Jensen, then headed home.

Go inside, came another word from our Lord while I was driving past The Holy Name of Mary Church. There hung upon the building a large banner with these words from Hebrews 13:8: Jubilee 2000, Jesus Christ . . . Yesterday, today, and forever. With great anticipation I went in. Instantly my eyes focused upon a suspended crucifix. In reverence I knelt in their softly lit house of worship, and prayed.

Afterward I sat, then looked about. Suddenly a blue hymnal entitled *Journey Songs* got my attention. Hmm, I thought, wondering if "Morning Has Broken" was inside. So I laid it open in my lap, reached for eyeglasses, then looked downward. Oh, my God! I exclaimed silently, not wanting to disturb a man seated up front. The page had opened to selection 397 . . . "Morning Has Broken." On its adjoining page there was a song entitled "O How Blest." That selection describes perfectly this Holy Spirit moment.

Thank you, Lord, I prayed. Then, after silently singing "Morning Has Broken," I headed for the door. But just as I reached the outer threshold, The Holy Name of Mary's church bells sounded. Right at that moment a priest walked by. "They rang just as I stepped outside," I said in wonderment.

"They're ringing for you," the priest said in a teasing manner. "Listen," he added, "the Lutheran bells are ringing!" (I later recalled that some of our village churches ring their bells every day beginning at noon.) Then, after a short discussion with the priest about their doors being open all day to welcome in Christ, I shared the blessings that had been given inside their sanctuary. Lastly I told him about *In The Forest of Your Remembrance*, then asked for his name. "Father Matthew," he replied.

All of a sudden I felt it necessary to purchase another *Gifts of Grace*. Afterward, just as I was getting into my car, our Lord spoke again: Go back into the church; you didn't look at the statues. Lord, I've never given much attention to statues, I thought. But there must be something you want me to learn. First I went toward a life-size figure of a woman. It was closest to the pew where I had been sitting. Who is she? I wondered. In her hands lay an opened book. Below, a child was gazing at her face with a look of expectation. "Gift of Saint Anne's Lodge" read its plaque.

All of a sudden I heard our Lord again in the stillness: See the words written in her book. Then with complete joy I read: "A bud will blossom from the root of Jesse." O Lord, I wondered, will "Jesse's Tree" and "Jesse's Cloud" be published? Suddenly I felt compelled to enter a small alcove. There stood a lovely representation of the Virgin Mary. It greatly resembled the painting of our Lord's mother on *Gifts of Grace*. Thank you, Lord, I prayed, for revealing Saint Ann, your grandmother, and your mother, Mary, as mother to all. Finally, with renewed hope for future tellings, I went home knowing that my mourning days for unpublished works were over.

Later that day I shared this telling with a salesperson at the White Dove Christian Book Store. "Holy Name of Mary is my parish!" said Matthew. Several months later I discovered that a plaque is mounted high above the bell tower door in The Holy Name of Mary Church's vestibule. It says: "These chimes ring to the Glory of God." Thank you, Lord Jesus, I prayed silently, for keeping your servant humble.

PSALMS 63:1–3 (KJV) *O God, thou art my God; early will I seek thee: My soul thirsteth for thee, my flesh longeth for thee in a dry and thirsty land, where no water is; To see thy power and thy glory, so as I have seen thee in the sanctuary. Because thy lovingkindness is better than life, my lips shall praise thee.*

Step Up a Level Higher

LUKE 22:31–32 (NKJV) *And the Lord said, "Simon, Simon! Indeed, Satan has asked for you, that he may sift you as wheat. But I have prayed for you, that your faith should not fail; and when you have returned to Me, strengthen your brethren."*

It was the first thing that I heard upon waking: a still, small voice from within. Step up a level higher, said our Lord. Maybe I should work upstairs today, I concluded. So that morning I didn't go to Sunflower, my workplace that is in a wooded area outside our home. But after a few hours of unfruitful work I came to the realization that our God had something else in mind. What, I wondered, could it be? His answer came a few days later.

"Let's meet in the third car," I told our youngest son, Myles, as we talked on the telephone. We were making plans to attend a panel discussion on children's books that was being held at the Society of Illustrators Club in New York City. "Oh, no!" I exclaimed on the way to Croton–Harmon railroad station. I had neglected to get money out of the bank, and had only one check and a credit card. If I stop at the bank, I thought, it will cause me to miss spending time with Myles.

Keep going, came a message from our Lord. I'll supply all of your needs. Thank you, I thought. Moments later, when I was passing by a local fruit stand, a solution came. Cash the check, said our Lord. Immediately I parked.

"Hi, Gloria," I said excitedly, greeting its proprietor. "Can you cash a check for me?"

"Sure, sweetie," she responded with her usual smile. "How much do you need?" I asked her for thirty dollars, not wanting to deplete her cash drawer. Then I thanked her and headed for the station with a feeling of relief. But having to use cash for parking and a round-trip ticket (because credit cards are not accepted), I boarded the train to New York City with an almost empty wallet.

"Don't worry, Mom," Myles said when I joined him on the train. "I have enough cash for both of us." I felt better, but not comfortable.

Upon our arrival in New York we headed for an uptown subway. "Look, Myles," I said as we approached the cashier's window. "A billfold!" Sure enough, a brand-new leather billfold lay at my feet. There was no identification tag inside it, and it held five dollars. "Look what the Lord has done!" I exclaimed. "He knew that I was worried, so he gave me this money."

Our son looked dubious. "I don't think so, Mom," he said. "Maybe you should turn it over to a cashier. The person who lost it may come back."

I shook my head. "Myles," I responded, "you're wrong. Anyway," I added, "the cashier would probably keep it." Feeling at ease with my estimation of the situation, I put the billfold inside my purse. Moments later I found a subway pass. However, after attempting to pay my fare with it, I learned the pass was invalid. Myles just shook his head.

Then a few blocks from the Society, he and I stopped to eat. All through the meal I tried to convince him that a gift had been given. However, our son remained steadfast in his belief. Afterward, we came upon a homeless man sitting on the sidewalk.

Right away I took out a dollar. "No, Mom," said our son, giving me a handful of change. But, unbeknown to us, three dollars had fallen from Myles's pocket.

"Hey, mister," called the homeless person, "you're losing your money." I reached down and picked the bills up off the sidewalk.

"Give all of it to him, Mom," Myles said. I handed the money to the grateful person. Even then I was spiritually blind to what our Lord was trying to teach. I should have turned the bill-fold in at the cashier's window when I had the opportunity. It didn't belong to me. But I hadn't as of yet come to that awakening. I went home believing that the five dollars had been left there for me.

That next afternoon, I went to The Art Barn in Ossining, New York, to purchase a gift for a friend. Moments after arriving home, I needed my eyeglasses but I couldn't find my purse. Right then a beep interrupted Jerry's telephone conversation. "Mr. Pinkney," said a woman caller, "this is The Art Barn. We found your phone number on a check in your wife's bag. We're holding it here for her."

At first my heart turned a somersault when recalling that Jerry's gold watch, my antique watch, cellular phone, checks, and cash were inside. But deep within I felt that all was well. For I guessed that the spirit of our Lord was handling this situation, and teaching me a lesson. Forgive me, I prayed while driving back to the store. Sure enough, all of my belongings were there.

Then, just to make certain that I had learned well, two days later another lesson came. Jerry and I were appearing at a library in Portland, Oregon, when a brand-new sterling silver pin (in the likeness of a tree) disappeared from my jacket. Jerry had given it to me for my birthday. "You'll never find that beautiful pin," someone said. However, my guide for the evening decided to check the lost and found. To everyone's delight, my pin had been anonymously turned in. Then I told our hosts what the Lord had done.

"As soon as I get back to the hotel, I'm going to call our son and tell him that I was wrong," I told Jerry and the library staff.

"Myles," I said later when he picked up the phone, "you were right and I was wrong. I should have turned in that billfold." But it was too late for me to do that now. So I said, "I'm going to put five dollars in that wallet and give it to the next homeless person I meet."

Myles paused for a moment. "Mom," he responded, "I think you should put ten dollars in it." This time his mother listened. At last my eyes, my ears, and my heart were open to the truth. Thank you, Lord, for correcting me gently.

Later that night, on the way from the library to our hotel, a homeless person singled me out among Jerry and our hosts who were accompanying us. It was a startling moment. "Lady," he said, extending an open hand, "I haven't had anything to eat all day. Can you spare some change?" I stopped in my tracks. Jerry and our escorts started across the street.

"I certainly can," I replied, searching for the billfold that was at the bottom of my evening purse.

"Come on, Gloria," Jerry called with an alarmed tone in his voice. Finally, the billfold was retrieved. So I laid it in the palm of the man's hand. He stood as if frozen to the sidewalk, staring at his hand, then up at me. I waited for a second, then hurried to join the others.

"Hey, lady," the man called as we walked away, "thanks!"

JOHN 13:34–35 (TEV) *"And now I give you a new commandment: love one another. As I have loved you, so you must love one another. If you have love for one another, then everyone will know that you are my disciples."*

Wow, Lord!

JOHN 7:17–18 (NWT) *If anyone desires to do His will, he will know concerning the teaching whether it is from God or I speak of my own originality. He that speaks of his own originality is seeking his own glory; but he that seeks the glory of Him that sent him, this one is true, and there is no unrighteousness in him.*

One day while standing in a checkout line at a local supermarket, I overheard an elderly woman telling the cashier about her failing health. Instantly I prayed an intercessory prayer, then asked the Holy Spirit if I should speak to her. Right away an affirmative feeling came. "Pardon me," I began, "I couldn't help overhearing the conversation about your health." The woman turned with a little smile on her face.

"There is a church in town with a welcoming banner whose doors are open all day," I said, "called Holy Name of Mary. You could go there to pray for a healing," I suggested. The woman's smile grew. "God is working miracles in that place," I told her.

"But," she replied, "I'm Jewish, and it's a Catholic church. Do you think it's all right if I go in there?"

"Well," I responded, "I'm Baptist, but our Lord has blessed me every time I have entered Holy Name of Mary's sanctuary."

"There's a little annex near my home in Harmon," the woman told me, "Chapel of the Good Shepherd. I'll go there!" she said.

Then, with a broadened smile, she took her grocery bag and left. Thank you, Lord, I prayed silently.

A few days later as I was waiting at a traffic light in Harmon, our Lord's still, small voice gently spoke: Find the Chapel of the Good Shepherd. So I turned because I knew there was a church at the next intersection. However, I didn't know its name. Suddenly something on my left got my attention. To my delight, there, surrounded by yellowing shrubs stood a dazzling white marble statue of Christ Jesus. He was basking in sunlight with outstretched arms, and a heart upon his breast. "Thank you, Lord," I said, "for leading me to your chapel." Then I noticed the self-same welcoming banner as the one hanging at The Holy Name of Mary Church. So I parked, then stepped inside.

Except for the sound of trickling water from a fountain, the sanctuary was still. Only the Spirit of our Lord and I were present that day. Then, with a bowed head, I passed through its vestibule, looked for an opened kneeling bench, knelt, and prayed. Afterward, I sat with an incredible feeling of peace, then looked up toward the altar. "Wow, Lord!" I exclaimed. There lay a blue Advent cloth with one word and four lit white candles stitched upon it. In utter astonishment I read, "Gloria."

Now, the word *Gloria* is often used within holy songs, but I had never seen it written upon an altar cloth. "Lord," I said, remembering the Apostle Peter's response when he, along with James and John, were on the mountain with our Savior, "it is wonderful to be here." Instantly I knew within my heart why I was there. Thank you, Lord, I prayed. I'll go get Gloria Nicole from school.

"There is something that I want you to see, Gloria," I said as she got into my car. My granddaughter looked curious, but didn't ask for an explanation. So while she took a short nap, I headed for the chapel. Lord, may this day be a blessing, I silently prayed while parking. Gloria is going to be so surprised!

However, as soon as we approached the door, my granddaughter's face lit up. "It says Gloria in there!" she exclaimed. The fourteen-year-old had looked straight through a door pane and had spotted the blue altar cloth. Amazing, I thought, as we prayed within the sanctuary. Why didn't I see it right away?

Afterward we stopped at the statue of Christ, then read the prayer engraved at his feet, entitled "Give Us Your Heart."

> Give us, Lord, a pure heart for loving:
> A heart of flesh, not one of stone;
> To love God and men.
> Give us your own heart, to love really, forgetting ourselves.
> Someone has to transplant your heart in place of ours
> which functions so poorly when it comes to LOVING
> others.
> Let it be you, Lord, loving through us.
> Give us your heart to love the Father,
> Give us your heart to love Mary our Mother,
> Give us your heart to love your brothers and sisters—
> they are ours too—
> To love those who have gone to heaven and to love also
> those right beside us here on earth.

"Mom-Mom," said Gloria Nicole as soon as we got back into my car, "I want to ask a question." Instantly I put my vehicle in park. "Was the name *Gloria* on that cloth about you or me?"

I gave her an understanding smile. "It wasn't about either of us," I answered. "Do you remember that our name means 'praise God'? Gloria nodded her head. "This is a reminder from the Holy Spirit," I explained, that "we must always *glorify God*, and not ourselves."

Later I learned that the general theme of the Jubilee Year Banner is "Open Wide the Doors to Christ: Evangelize, Reconcile, Celebrate!" Also, it is of importance to note that our Lord Jesus sent me to his chapel just a few days before the blue cloth was to be replaced by a white one in celebration of the Christmas season.

ISAIAH 55:12–13 (NJB) *Yes, you will go out with joy and be led away in safety. Mountains and hills will break into joyful cries before you and all the trees of the countryside clap their hands. Cypress will grow instead of thorns, myrtle instead of nettles. And this will be fame for Yahweh, an eternal monument never to be effaced.*

REFELECTIONS

My son, do not forget my law, But let your heart keep my commands, For length of days and long life And peace they will add to you. Let not mercy and truth forsake you; Bind them around your neck, Write them on the tablet of your heart, And so find favor and high esteem in the sight of God and man. Trust in the LORD with all your heart, And lean not on your own understanding; In all your ways acknowledge Him, And He shall direct your paths.

PROVERBS 3:1–6
(NKJV)

Goodly News Reflections

HABAKKUK 2:2–3 (NKJV) *Then the LORD answered me and said: "Write the vision And make it plain on tablets, That he may run who reads it. For the vision is yet for an appointed time; But at the end it will speak, and it will not lie. Though it tarries, wait for it; Because it will surely come, It will not tarry."*

If only I could say that I was never overwhelmed while striving to have a third manuscript published. *Best Street in the World* was to have been a chapter book about Ernestine, the young heroine in my first publication. However, after two years of struggling with a fictional accounting of my mother's death when I was eight, my editor, Phyllis Fogelman, deemed it wise for me to put that manuscript aside. Afterward I worked on six more ideas without success.

"Yes ... my dear hearers," as my great-grandfather Reverend N.O. Thompson was known to begin a summation, there have been trials. Yet, my unwavering faith in our Lord Jesus Christ, like my ancestors', and the daily refreshings given by the Holy Spirit have sustained me as I continued to wait for our God's appointed time.

Then in 1998 I awoke early one morning to the sound of a still, small voice. In the forest of your remembrance, said our Lord the Holy Spirit. Immediately I got up. Write it down or you'll forget, I thought. In the forest of my remembrance, I wrote, then recalled what I had heard. Promptly I changed the word *my* to *your*. It's a title for my readers! I concluded. Now folks will see that the events in their lives that they believe to be small-world incidents, luck, or coincidence are you, Lord. I had been graced with a new title.

However, I had not finished rewriting what I had been working on. So I went back to it. "Lord," I cried one day, after another unfruitful attempt at obtaining a contract, "please tell me what you would have me write." Then, as always, with shut eyes and both hands upon my *Spirit-Filled Life Bible* (the New King James Version), I opened my book, and with eyes wide open I read the heading on page 1388: "A Book of Remembrance, Malachi 3:16. Then those who feared the LORD spoke to one another, And the LORD listened and heard them; So a book of remembrance was written before Him For those who fear the LORD And who meditate on His name."

"Oh, thank you, precious Father, Son, and Holy Spirit," I exclaimed. "*In the Forest of Your Remembrance* it is." I had just received, for the first time in my life, an instant answer from our Lord. He was calling me, Gloria, to write true narratives about his signposts, wonders, and miracles in my life.

Now, you may ask, "What brought you this gift?" It is by the grace of our merciful God. Also, I believe the prayers of my great-aunt Alma have been answered. She raised me in Philadelphia after my mother died, and from the time I was eight until I was eighteen she called out to God nightly on my behalf.

"Oh, Lord," she'd say with uplifted arms, "please let me live long enough to see this youngun marry a good man and make something of herself." To my aunt, making something of oneself meant living the life of a willing worker for Jesus.

Aunt Alma was a good and faithful servant. "Dear Lord," I prayed daily while growing up as an only child, "please give me a husband who will love me. Please let me have four kids; two boys and two girls." (Our Lord gave us one daughter and three sons.) Great-Aunt and I spent Sunday mornings in my first church home, Emmanuel Institutional Baptist, where, at age twelve, I experienced a visitation from the Holy Spirit. I can still recall his presence within me when I accepted our Lord Jesus Christ as my personal Savior, and was soon baptized. I didn't know it then, but that was the beginning of a pilgrimage that would eventually lead to a personal fellowship with our Lord the Holy Spirit.

I met Jerry, a senior and a commercial art student, at a high school Valentine's Day dance. When I brought him home, Aunt Alma said, "He's the one!" I didn't think so, but she was right. Three years later Jerry and I married, then moved to Boston. As soon as we were settled in Boston, I joined Ebenezer Baptist. However, when our family moved to the suburbs, I ceased going to a house of worship. Yet whenever life's struggles arose—and they did—I prayed. Also, there is no doubt in my mind that Great-Aunt never stopped until the day she fell asleep in Christ.

In 1970 we moved to New York and I began working closely with Jerry. Three years later the children and I joined The Star of Bethlehem Missionary Baptist, my third church. Yet it took me almost two decades to make a daily commitment to the studying of God's word.

Now, I began *In the Forest of Your Remembrance* feeling as if I were a wayfarer on a pilgrimage. Yet from the beginning of my journey, our Creator God has provided instructions in his Holy Bible; through his Son, Jesus, and the Holy Spirit.

At first I was confused about our God's plan for this book. For example: On November 6, 1997, I spoke at the William F. Laman Public Library in North Little Rock, Arkansas. My subject was the writing of my first two books. On that visit I told audiences that "both were based on real experiences with a little fiction added."

Afterward, at a question-and-answer period, a young boy who was seated up front was first to raise his hand. "Are you ever going to write the truth?" he asked. After recouping from the message in the child's words, I spoke of future plans to tell stories based on my family's ministry in the Carolinas.

Then, later that evening, another eye-opening experience came from a man who stood through the length of my presentation. He also had his hand up first. "Are you ever going to write about Jesus Christ?" the man asked. I repeated my earlier response. Lord, I wondered, what is happening? Yet, deep inside I knew his answer.

After this encounter with two messengers from our Father God, it's hard for me to understand why, when beginning this book, I was hesitant to call our Lord, the Son—Jesus—by name. My intent was to write thirty-three true tellings with universal appeal. Then, very early one morning, I awoke hearing a soft voice. Will Christ be revealed? asked the Holy Spirit. "Yes, Lord," I answered.

Months later, while nearing the end of this manuscript, I received another directive while I was making an author visit at a school in Harlem, New York. A parent came to visit between presentations. I soon learned that one of her daughters had been in a serious accident. Right away she and I began talking about our Creator God, and the power of prayer. Our beliefs were not identical, however, our love and trust in one God were shared. I noticed that the woman had a scarf on her head, but I was not immediately aware that she was of the Muslim faith.

On my way home I was guided by the Spirit to stop at a bookstore. "Do you have The Koran?" I asked a salesperson. She led me to a shelf with three different publications. Lord, I prayed silently, please let me know if this is your will. Then I reached for one. Immediately I felt drawn to its russet-colored jacket. "Yes!"

I exclaimed upon spotting my publisher's logo on its cover. Thank you, Lord, I prayed, for a clear signpost. I needed to be absolutely certain.

How wonderful it is to end this part of reflections with good news about the injured girl in Harlem. Her mother and I shared a spiritual heritage, and were in one accord with our Lord God. Things are back to normal, a teacher wrote in response to my note.

"Hallelujah!" I exclaimed.

PSALM 40:5 (NKJV) *Many, O LORD my God, are Your wonderful works Which You have done; And Your thoughts toward us cannot be recounted to You in order; If I would declare and speak of them, they are more than can be numbered.*

Spiritual Reflections

JOB 28:28 (NKJV) *And to man He said, "Behold, the fear of the Lord, that is wisdom, And to depart from evil is understanding."*

One morning in November of the year 2000, just before daybreak, a message came. This is the way that pleases God, said a still, small voice. I had been lying in bed thinking about how to best end this book. The same words had been given months earlier, but I wanted to use it for a new telling. Then part of a verse from John 14:6 entered my thoughts. "I am the way, the truth and the life." Right then I knew what to do. "The reflections must glorify Father, Son, and Holy Spirit," I told Jerry, "and show the spiritual heritage of all people."

Then I remembered that a teacher in Peekskill, New York, had given me a book about the Amish at an author visit. "Lord," I inquired, "is this your will for the good news tellings?" An answer was given a short time later when I encountered a group of young Amish women. So when I opened my Amish book, three words got my attention, plain and simple.

Weeks later I made a decision to use John's gospel (beloved disciple of Jesus) from the *Good News Bible: Today's English Version*, to explain the Holy Spirit verses. These plain and simple writings would make it easier for parents to teach the sacred text to children.

The Unbelief of the People
JOHN 12:37–43

Even though he had performed all these miracles in their presence, they did not believe in him, so that what the prophet Isaiah had said might come true:

> *"Lord, who believed the message we told?*
> *To whom did the Lord reveal his power?"*
> *And so they were not able to believe, because Isaiah also said,*
> *"God has blinded their eyes*
> *and closed their minds,*
> *so that their eyes would not see,*
> *and their minds would not understand,*
> *and they would not turn to me,*
> *says God,*
> *for me to heal them."*

Isaiah said this because he saw Jesus' glory and spoke about him.

Even then, many Jewish authorities believed in Jesus; but because of the Pharisees they did not talk about it openly, so as not to be expelled from the synagogue. They loved human approval rather than the approval of God.

Jesus the Way to the Father
JOHN 14:1–14

"Do not be worried and upset," Jesus told them. "Believe in God and believe also in me. There are many rooms in my Father's house, and I am going to prepare a place for you. I would not tell you this if it were not so. And after I go and prepare a place for you, I will come back and take you to myself, so that you will be where I am. You know the way that leads to the place where I am going."

Thomas said to him, "Lord, we do not know where you are going; so how can we know the way to get there?"

Jesus answered him, "I am the way, the truth, and the life; no one goes to the Father except by me. Now that you have known me," he said to them, "you will know my Father also, and from now on you do know him and you have seen him."

Philip said to him, "Lord, show us the Father; that is all we need."

Jesus answered, "For a long time I have been with you all; yet you do not know me, Philip? Whoever has seen me has seen the Father. Why, then, do you say, 'Show us the Father'? Do you not believe, Philip, that I am in the Father and the Father is in me? The words that I have spoken to you," Jesus said to his disciples, "do not come from me. The Father, who remains in me, does his own work. Believe me when I say that I am in the Father and the Father is in me. If not believe because of the things I do. I am telling you the truth: those who believe in me will do what I do—yes, they will do even greater things, because I am going to the Father. And I will do whatever you ask for in my name, so that the Father's glory will be shown through the Son. If you ask me for anything in my name, I will do it.

The Promise of the Holy Spirit
JOHN 14:15–31

"If you love me, you will obey my commandments. I will ask the Father, and he will give you another Helper, who will stay with you forever. He is the Spirit, who reveals the truth about God. The world cannot receive him, because it cannot see him or know him. But you know him, because he remains with you and is in you.

"When I go, you will not be left all alone. I will come back to you. In a little while the world will see me no more, but you will see me; and because I live, you also will live. When that day comes, you will know that I am in my Father and that you are in me, just as I am in you.

"Those who accept my commandments and obey them are the ones who love me. My Father will love those who love me; I too will love them and reveal myself to them."

Judas (not Judas Iscariot) said, "Lord, how can it be that you will reveal yourself to us and not to the world?"

Jesus answered him, "Those who love me will obey my teaching. My Father will love them, and my Father and I will come to them and live with them. Those who do not love me do not obey my teaching. And the teaching you have heard is not mine, but comes from the Father, who sent me.

"I have told you this while I am still with you. The Helper, the Holy Spirit, whom the Father will send in my name, will teach you everything and make you remember all that I have told you.

"Peace is what I leave with you; it is my own peace that I give you. I do not give it as the world does. Do not be worried and upset; do not be afraid. You heard me say to you, 'I am leaving, but I will come back to you.' If you loved me, you would be glad that I am going to the Father; for he is greater than I. I have told you this now before it all happens, so that when it does happen, you will believe. I cannot talk with you much longer, because the ruler of this world is coming. He has no power over me, but the world must know that I love the Father; that is why I do everything as he commands me.

"Come, let us go from this place."

The Coming of the Holy Spirit
ACTS 2:1—4

When the day of Pentecost came, all the believers were gathered together in one place. Suddenly there was a loud noise from the sky which sounded like a strong wind blowing, and it filled the whole house where they were sitting. Then they saw what looked like tongues of fire which spread out and touched each person there. They were all filled with the Holy Spirit and began to talk in other languages, as the Spirit enabled them to speak.

Conclusion
JOHN 21:25

Now, there are many other things that Jesus did. If they were all written down one by one, I suppose the whole world could not hold the books that would be written.

JUDE 1:24—25 (NKJV) *Now to Him who is able to keep you from stumbling, And to present you faultless Before the presence of His glory with exceeding joy, To God our Savior, Who alone is wise, Be glory and majesty, Dominion and power, Both now and forever. Amen.*

About the Artists

JERRY PINKNEY created his art for this book using pencil and watercolors on paper. He has been illustrating children's books since 1964 and has the rare distinction of being the recipient of four Caldecott Honor Medals—in 2000 for *The Ugly Duckling*, in 1995 for *John Henry* by Julius Lester, in 1990 for *The Talking Eggs* by Robert D. San Souci, and in 1989 for *Mirandy and Brother Wind* by Patricia C. McKissack. He has won the Coretta Scott King Award four times, and the Coretta Scott King Honor twice, among other awards. In addition Jerry Pinkney is a successful artist whose work has been exhibited at many prestigious museums and other venues. He and his wife, Gloria Jean, the author, live in Westchester County, New York.

BRIAN PINKNEY created his illustrations in scratchboard. He has illustrated numerous books for children, including *Seven Candles for Kwanzaa* by his wife, Andrea Davis Pinkney, and has received two Caldecott Honors—in 1999 for *Duke Ellington*, also by Andrea Davis Pinkney, and in 1996 for *The Faithful Friend* by Robert D. San Souci. Among Brian Pinkney's books that he both wrote and illustrated is *The Adventures of Sparrowboy*, the winner of the 1997 *Boston Globe–Horn Book* Award. He has also received a Coretta Scott King Award and three Coretta Scott King Honors. He lives with Andrea and their children in Brooklyn, New York.

MYLES C. PINKNEY took black-and-white photographs for his mother's book. He is a freelance photographer whose work has appeared in magazines and newspapers. In 2001 Myles and his wife, Sandra, were presented with the NAACP Image Award for Children's Literature for their book *Shades of Black*. Myles Pinkney's other children's books include *Sitting Pretty* by Dinah Johnson and *It's Raining Laughter* by Nikki Grimes. He lives with Sandra and their children in Poughkeepsie, New York.